Guardians of the Solar Shield

Earth's Climate Mirrors Under Attack

2029-2037

Sam Bleicher

Strategic Path Press
Winchester, Virginia

Guardians of the Solar Shield

Earth's Climate Mirrors Under Attack 2029-2037

by Sam Bleicher

ISBN # 978-0-9890093-4-8 Trade Paperback

Novels by Sam Bleicher

GUARDIANS OF THE SOLAR SHIELD
Earth's Climate Mirrors Under Attack
2029-2037

THE PLOT TO COOL THE PLANET, A Novel
Newman Springs Publishing
April 22, 2019, revised and reprinted May 2020
An Indie Excellence Book Awards Finalist

APPOINTMENTS,
A Novel of Politics in Our Nation's Capital
Strategic Path Press 2013
under the pseudonym David Carmell

I dedicate this book to those who will be alive in 2037 and all those planning for that future today.

I hope this story stimulates your imagination about the prospects and perils of the world to come and persuades humans everywhere to work on preserving what we can of Earth and its living inhabitants.

Sam Bleicher

Part I

Chapter 1

A New Beginning

22 APRIL 2032. THE GLEAMING white SpaceX rocket begins its ponderous, thundering ascent from the NASA Johnson Space Center in Houston, Texas, into a synchronous Earth orbit. Fifty minutes later, it releases its payload of 20 solar mirror capsules. A few days later, the final 20 of the 480 Solar Shield mirrors, designed to generate electricity and slow the global warming already devastating large parts of the planet.

The United Nations Solar Shield Project, or SSP, was on schedule from an engineering standpoint. But it was a decade too late to undo the relentless damage already caused by the Earth's overheating. Severe storms more frequently generated floods that destroyed cities and essential food crops. Disintegration of the polar icecaps was inexorably drowning urban centers and coastal farms. Droughts were turning farmlands and forests into deserts.

Together these conditions had produced millions of climate refugees with no place to go and no opportunity to become self-sufficient. The SSP could only hope to mitigate the further destruction waiting ahead without this concrete human intervention to deflect a small percentage of the Sun's energy.

Commander Robert Fauré of the SSP Corps (SSPC) explained to the world the importance of this milestone for all of Earth's living inhabitants—human, plant, and animal.

"The Solar Shield Project promises to slow the rate of climate disruption dramatically. But this massive effort is far from a cure-all. It only buys us time to complete the transformation to carbon-free energy systems and begin reducing the carbon imbalance in our atmosphere.

"We must remember — if we think this program solves the climate crisis and do nothing else, further disasters will engulf us all."

Lieutenant Kelly O'Rourke watched the launch with fascination from her small office at Casement Aerodrome, the Irish Air Force headquarters. Her eyes sparkled with enthusiasm as she listened to Commander Fauré.

She immediately videocalled Maureen. The youngest of four children, Kelly relied on her oldest sister for advice on everything.

"Hi, sis! How is everyone today?"

"We're all fine. I just returned from grocery shopping. It gets more complicated as the kids grow up. They all have opinions about what is edible. How are you?"

"Excited. I hope you watched the Solar Shield rocket launch. I'd love to be part of that project. Reducing climate disruption is a mission worthy of a lifetime. I'm thinking maybe I could transfer to the UN Space Shield Project Command. I'd be part of something important, not just pushing paper in this backwater. And I'd live in New York City! I'll never have that kind of life here. What do you think, sis?"

Maureen laughed.

"Slow down, Kelly. Let's think this through. You've been preparing yourself for a decade to serve in the Irish Air Force—a college degree with honors in aeronautical engineering, flying lessons in your spare time, and the grueling military training program, complete with physical self-defense, small arms use and safety, and crawling under barbed wire with live fire overhead.

"I know you're disappointed you didn't pass the final flying test. But why would you throw away a secure desk job here to go to a desk job in New York, away from everyone you know?"

Kelly was frustrated by this mundane advice. "Sis, you don't appreciate what I'm facing here. I was on my way to being a top gun pilot, which would have made me something special in the Irish Air Force.

"I blew it for a single night of sex with a guy in my class I hardly knew. I was lonely. The Plan B pills worked, but they left me with a week of morning sickness at the wrong time.

"Flying upside down in the final flight tests was unbearable. I asked for a second chance, but I couldn't explain why without exposing my misconduct. I couldn't do that to him or me.

"Meanwhile, the guy passed the tests and became a pilot, even though he had violated the 'no sex during pilot training' rule just as much as I had.

"So here I am in a desk job with no prospects of ever rising above the level of a glorified clerk. I'm already known here as the hotshot wannabe who couldn't fly upside down. It's deadly."

"My darling Kelly, there's no great shame in being unable to fly upside down. Your senior commanders recognize your extraordinary energy and intelligence, and they have given you a safe, secure administrative position. You'll have a stable career with regular promotions.

"You've told me that the pilots are mostly just observing the new self-directed drones in action anyway. Now you won't need to be apprehensive about losing your mental or physical acuity. Or about paying your rent. Maybe you'll eventually find someone worth marrying."

"Not here at Casement," Kelly shot back. But she instantly softened her response. Maureen was her only confidant. "Okay, I see your point. But I'm going to explore the Space Shield Corps possibility. I'll keep you informed. Please don't say anything to Dad or anyone else; this fantasy probably won't ever happen.

"Give my love to everyone. I'll try to come visit one of these days soon." Kelly quickly ended the call before she lost her temper at her sister's narrow vision of life.

Visiting home, only a two-hour drive, was a promise routinely made but kept once in a blue moon. Being the little kid in the family forever just brought back the rebellious feelings of her teenage years.

Kelly dreaded being a desk-bound bureaucrat in a minuscule air force of fewer than 800 officers, where pilots were the only heroes. The first six months at her desk job confirmed her unhappiness. The administrative staff were just so much wallpaper to the pilots and senior officers.

Kelly talked to her immediate superior the next day about transferring to the SSPC. He was quietly happy to send her off in a new direction. Less impressed by her acknowledged talents than his superiors, he found her too restless, too ambitious, and too dissatisfied with her assignments.

"If you think you would be happier at the SSPC in New York City, I'll do what I can for you. It might be a better fit."

The transfer didn't happen quickly. It wasn't until May 2033 that the SSPC informed Kelly of her conditional acceptance. SSPC recruits all began with a two-year probationary assignment. Kelly would join the November class of recruits. She eagerly called Maureen.

"They accepted me! In November, I'll be reporting for work at the Solar Shield Corps in Manhattan! It's a chance to start over, this time in a worldwide organization with a new and challenging mission. I can hardly wait!"

Maureen feared Kelly was on a path to another disappointment. But there was no dissuading her now.

"Congratulations! I hope it's everything you wish for. I'm sure you'll find New York City fascinating, even if the job isn't exciting. But please be cautious. Lots of hustlers work on newcomers to New York City. You can't trust anyone. And don't forget, you can always come home. We'll be happy to have you back."

"Do you want me to tell Mom and Dad the news?"

Kelly thought for a moment. There were no appealing alternatives.

"I need to tell Dad myself, but you could lay some groundwork. I've never told them about failing the flying test or that I hate my desk job. If you give them that background, maybe they won't be so shocked when I say I'm off to New York City."

"I can do that. But you really must come home for a few days and see them before you go. Dad's not getting any younger. I'd like to see you myself, and the kids are old enough to miss you. Kilbride isn't so far away, you know."

"I promise I'll do it this time. And maybe you'll all come to visit me in New York once I'm settled in."

With gritted teeth, Kelly arranged to visit Maureen and her siblings and parents. Having been alerted that Kelly was leaving for New York, everyone was supportive and warm.

Dad and Mom were uneasy about her being alone in that enormous city in a foreign country. They had hoped she satisfied her wanderlust in her unstructured sojourns in Europe in college. They buried their concerns behind a cheery face, wished her well, and repeatedly reminded her she was welcome here, whatever the circumstances.

Kelly was comforted by their warmth. She grew a bit sentimental, now that she was leaving Ireland, possibly for good. She and Maureen had pleasant conversations over lunch and a long walk. For the first time, she felt she was an adult member of the family, not just the little kid. The good feelings freed her enthusiasm for what lay ahead.

∞∞∞

Wang Shu, Director of United Nations Security Management Services (SMS), watched the SpaceX launch in the comfort of her apartment across Manhattan from UN Headquarters. She had taken the SMS position in New York in 2026, declining to pursue a promising academic and political career in her native Singapore.

That same year, Mohamed Ibrahim, the Maldives Ambassador to the UN and the United States, passed up the opportunity to return home with his wife and children to Malé, the Maldives capital, to serve as Foreign Minister. Instead, he accepted a World Bank Vice-Presidency in Washington, D.C., dedicated to aiding tropical island states.

These career moves allowed Wang and Ibrahim to spend nights together frequently in New York without public attention. Despite their divergent cultural backgrounds, Wang and Ibrahim had been lovers since they met at a UNESCO Conference in Paris in 2014.

Marriage was out of the question. Ibrahim was s married Muslim, and though polygamy is allowed in the Maldives, a Muslim man cannot legally marry a woman who is not Muslim, Christian, nor Jewish. Marriage to Wang Shu, a Han Chinese Confucian from Singapore, would be barred, even if his wife allowed it.

Professionally, a marriage could upend their careers. The UN and the World Bank are indifferent to interfaith and interracial marriages. But the political reality is that their governments nominate senior UN officials. Both would likely lose that endorsement by marrying a foreign diplomat, regardless of the spouse's religion.

Wang was eager to see Ibrahim this evening. His visits were always a pleasure, but the satellite launch made it a special event for both of them. The successful launch of the final set of SSP mirrors was a milestone on a path they had advocated for 15 years.

Wang prepared a memorable Middle Eastern repast. Creating sumptuous dinners and breakfasts that used no pork, a staple of the Chinese diet but forbidden to Muslims, was a challenge she always enjoyed. When Ibrahim arrived, she embraced him warmly and filled their champagne glasses. She offered a toast.

"Today, we see the fruits of our daring efforts years ago, risking our careers and possibly our lives to create a secret tropospheric chemical veil. It was your idea, and it worked to pause global warming just enough to demonstrate a constructive path to minimize climate disruption right now, not just for those who survive to the 22nd Century.

"Whether this new SSP ultimately succeeds in saving civilization or even a human remnant, it will reduce the suffering of millions alive today. That's more than most diplomats can say about their life's work."

Ibrahim responded, smiling affectionately.

"You deserve as much credit as I do. You are the one who persuaded Prime Minister Li to gamble Singapore's money and his family's political reputation on our project. You gambled your entire career on its success."

While enjoying the day's triumph, Ibrahim turned somber.

"We shouldn't assume everything will be smooth sailing from here on. The SSP can probably stabilize the climate on average, giving us more time to implement permanent solutions to excessive greenhouse gas emissions. But it won't stop the damage from rising sea levels flooding millions of homes or undo the deadly ocean acidification that is killing fish stocks everywhere. It's already too late to reverse those consequences. I don't know if the SSP will be able to save civilization."

Wang was surprised by the intensity of Ibrahim's foreboding. Somewhat deflated herself, she leaned forward and took his hand to comfort him.

"Could we have done any better?"

Ibrahim sank deeper into his chair and stared into space for a moment.

"I doubt it. But I'm not convinced the SSP's mirrors will protect the climate as well as our chemical veil did.

The mirrors have multiple, potentially conflicting missions. It's certainly not the cheapest way to block 2% of the solar energy reaching Earth, which is all we need to slow climate disruption.

The climate modelers and satellite engineers designed the SSP mirror system under enormous time pressure. They had only a theoretical understanding of the climate consequences of its reflectivity and shadows. They evaluated the impact as best they could, but they didn't consider everything.

"They seem to have overlooked entirely the impact of the mirror shadows on tropical tourism, which is entirely dependent on expectations of sunny weather. No one wants to schedule a convention in a place where the sky may be clear but gray every day and visitors can't sit in the sun or enjoy seeing shadows.

Unsure of what prompted Ibrahim's intense feelings, Wang interrupted. "Is tourism really that important?"

"In some places, yes. The Maldives is one of several island states that depend almost entirely on tourism for the marginal income that raises people above subsistence. It means electricity, the internet, and clean drinking water for the people.

"I'm already hearing from Maldives tourist resorts that rumors about the mirror shadows are undermining their business.

"There are other problems with the mirrors. Their global benefits far outweigh this potential damage. But no mechanism exists to compensate those who suffer adverse consequences.

"The technicians can probably realign a few mirrors to avoid adverse effects without reducing the whole system's benefits. But the legally prescribed process is long and slow. In the meantime, the resorts will go bankrupt without major bookings."

Wang quickly saw where these thoughts were leading. She led Ibrahim to the sofa and put her arm around him.

"Have you talked to Commander Fauré about this matter?"

"Not yet. It's awkward for an SSPC Board Member to behave like a lobbyist for his home country's tourist industry. A quick remedy would circumvent the legal procedures, even if Fauré is personally confident that it's a sound decision.

"The whole idea of responding to political or economic pressure or inside influence contradicts the UN's explicit promise of a transparent, scientific balancing of costs and benefits in SSP operations."

Wang's facile mind quickly envisioned the risks of any intervention by Ibrahim. She didn't hesitate to express her concerns.

"You might be endangering your reputation by pursuing this, and Commander Fauré's reputation could suffer even more if he does anything for you."

Ibrahim nodded; he also saw those risks.

"Yes, and it could undermine support for the whole SSP. But why serve on the Board if I can't help solve this practical difficulty? It certainly won't help the SSP if the Tropical Tourism Association mounts a public relations attack on the SSP. I can only hold them back if

I tell them I'm looking for an informal solution. And that means talking to Fauré.

"It isn't as if I'm asking him to implement some a nefarious scheme to punish a personal enemy or obtain geopolitical advantages for the Maldives. I just want to help a few resorts that provide a livelihood for people who would otherwise be mired in poverty."

Wang thought better of saying anything more. She had her own professional obligations as a UN official, and she didn't want to know what might happen next. She deftly redirected the conversation to more pleasant matters.

"It's time for dessert. I made a special pie for you." She collected the dishes and disappeared into the kitchen.

Ibrahim was equally happy to leave the SSP discussion behind. They ate Wang's pie with gusto.

Ibrahim was delighted. "Thank you for dinner. You know, it's wonderful to be here with you. You understand my world as well as I do, if not better. I'm always happier after I've spent a night in your embrace."

With that, they walked arm in arm to the bedroom for an evening of comforting love.

Chapter 2

Kelly Goes To Work

KELLY REPORTED FOR DUTY at SSPC Headquarters on 1 November 2033. Coming to New York three weeks early allowed her time to find a small apartment walking distance from the SSPC offices. McFadden's Saloon, a casual sports bar nearby, was becoming her fallback dinner spot. She made no effort to meet anyone and was grateful that others respected her privacy.

The sunny apartment was a little pricier than she expected, but her New York-based UN-scale SSPC salary made it affordable. The City had banned private passenger vehicles from most of Manhattan and the commercial areas in the other boroughs years before. She could walk to work most days and take a driverless taxi when necessary. She was still waiting to receive her Universal Identification Card, known as a UID, which electronically recorded her identity, citizenship and passport number, vaccination status, and authority to drive in the US state of residence.

She videocalled Maureen on 31 October to share her exhilaration with the life she was creating for herself.

"You can't imagine Manhattan! It isn't just that there are lots of tall buildings. The whole scale of the place is unbelievable, and the sense of energy is amazing. No one talks, thinks, or moves slowly. And people talk to strangers and help them! That alone changes the whole feeling of the City from what we see in the movies.

"The museums are incredible. Most of the art we studied online is located here and far more impressive than it could ever be on a screen. I love it here."

Maureen listened impatiently, already late for meetings with her children's teachers on Parents' Night. She was still apprehensive about her little sister's future in New York.

"That all sounds wonderful. I'm so glad things are going well so far! I can't talk right now; I'm late for a meeting at the kids' school. Please take care of yourself. Call again when you have a chance! We all love you and miss you! I'll want to know everything! Talk to you again soon."

Kelly tried not to feel rejected by the abrupt ending. She knew Maureen had a busy family life to manage. She didn't envy her hectic married life.

Kelly was also busy reading about the SSPC's creation. UN documents from 2025 to 2028 explained the system's rationale and design, but she could see they papered over genuine controversies and ambiguities.

The plan envisioned 480 reflector mirrors lined up over the Earth in equatorial geosynchronous orbits. The paper-thin mirrors would be made of a nanotechnology-based fabric designed to draw heat from the atmosphere below and push it out into space. They would be coated with a photoelectric film to generate electricity. Each mirror would be over three miles in diameter, with supporting struts to hold the fabric in place.

These 480 "umbrellas" would deflect about 2% of the solar energy coming to Earth, slowing global warming. Most of the electricity would be beamed by microwave to the International Space Station, the International Moon Base then under construction, and 48 Earth-based receiving stations. The SSP mirrors needed only a fraction of the electricity they produced—part of the project's fiscal appeal.

The SSPC Board of Directors selected Robert Fauré as SSPC Commander in 2029. His mission was to coordinate SSP operations as NASA launched the mirrors and placed them in orbit. Then the SSPC would take over operating the mirrors and dealing with any technical or political challenges and unanticipated consequences.

Fauré was fully aware of the precariousness of the fundamental global commitment to the SSP. The SSPC had to make it work, or the UN would cancel funding for it. He wisely selected a new building a short walk from UN Headquarters as his Headquarters. It allowed him easy access to other senior UN Secretariat personnel and ambassadors from interested UN Member States. This proximity gave him ample opportunity to explain and defend the SSP concept to the doubters and satisfy the bean-counters obsessed with proper cost management.

∞∞∞

Kelly was apprehensive as she reported for work. The day began with a routine "Welcome Meeting" for the 14 recruits joining that day.

"For those of you I have not met, I am Commander Robert Fauré, the leader of the SSPC. I want to welcome you to our team. I wish I could put each of you to work on an exciting project immediately, because there is plenty to be done.

"But the first six months of your time here will be devoted to learning our mission, our operational systems, and our organizational structure and procedures. I can't stress enough the importance of studying diligently for the Induction Examination. Both the SSP Manual and the SSPC Manual must be virtually committed to memory.

"Passing the Induction Examination is a prerequisite for entry into the corps. If you pass, your score will be a significant factor when we allocate work assignments. I have confidence you can all pass if you study diligently; otherwise, you wouldn't be here.

"Finally, let me introduce my Executive Assistant, Officer Sanjay Bhattachar. Jay was born in India but grew up and studied in Vancouver. He was a highly accomplished pilot in the Canadian Air Force, but he gave up that role when F-35 pilots became desk-bound operators of newer, high-performance drones. By 2026, the latest F-35s had been re-engineered to fly free of the constraints of human reaction times and pilot survival, which made them incredibly effective weapons. Flying became a desk job.

"Jay worked for me in the Canadian Air Force, and when I took this position, I eagerly brought him along. If you need anything from me, please talk to Jay to get on my calendar."

Jay offered a few welcoming remarks, including his contact information. The meeting adjourned, and the recruits spent the rest of the day filling in forms on health insurance and retirement benefits.

Kelly was excited to be part of the team. But her spirits fell when she realized her first six months must be devoted to memorizing the Manuals for the Induction Examination. She had already read them and felt confident she could already pass the exam.

Except for additional orientation sessions, she sat each day in a tiny, windowless beige cubicle, literally memorizing the two Manuals. They were available online, but each recruit received a hard copy.

The SSP Manual was a collection of minutiae about the design and operation of the Solar Shield mirrors. Studying them was about as exciting as learning an aircraft instruction manual.

Most of the SSPC Manual's content described the organization's structure and the personnel rules: conduct, pay grades, sick leave, vacation time, and retirement benefits—topics she hardly cared about right now.

Bill Adcock, the recruit in the adjoining cubicle, dropped by to discuss some of the more obscure points with Kelly. It was quickly evident that she understood the SSP far better than he did. He seemed more intent on developing a social relationship than on mastering the Manuals' intricacies.

Kelly shared an occasional lunch with Bill in the staff dining room when he invited her, and she asked him to join her at McFadden's Saloon once. She found him too shallow and dull to see often. One consequence was that she unwittingly gained a reputation among the male recruits as a cold fish and a nerd. She didn't mind.

In two months, Kelly could recite large parts of both Manuals from memory and instantly find anything else in her hard copy. She was not worried about passing the exam, which was "open book" and reputedly more exhausting than challenging.

Kelly's cubicle was one of 24 that aeronautical engineers had initially occupied. Each one held a wall displaying all the available data on the characteristics of 20 of the 480 mirrors. The engineer's task was to ensure the mirrors conformed to the SSP Master Plan specifications.

Six months after each launch, assuming no complications in the mirror's performance, the monitoring task was formally turned over to the "Multiple Solar Shield Tier-Y supercomputer," dubbed "MSTY" by the men and called "she" by everyone.

MSTY was the sole computer for all SSPC activities. She was a new-design, completely artificial-intelligence-based machine, so she began "stupid" but rapidly grew smarter than almost everyone. She managed mundane administrative chores like scheduling meetings, posting them on everyone's calendar, and proofreading everyone's draft memos.

More importantly, she continuously evaluated the sensor data from each mirror and matched it to "ground truth" data collected from the 48 ground stations and the Series 2 International Space Station. She constantly evaluated that information for internal consistency and conformity with the SSP Mission Statement and Master Plan.

The data on the 20 screens in Kelly's cubicle flowed endlessly—seven days a week, 24 hours a day—an Amazon River of data. MSTY stored it all in a capacious cloud drive. Kelly's outdated job description said she was solely responsible for reporting any inappropriate change in the data screens for Mirrors 160 through 179, the ones in her cubicle.

Performing that task conscientiously would require a recruit to learn the meaning of each number on the various screens, like "mean altitude," "perpendicular deviation," "instantaneous vertical acceleration," and "instantaneous horizontal acceleration."

But the recruits quickly realized that they were just duplicating MSTY's monitoring. Bill said most recruits considered their job descriptions obsolete and paid no attention to the data. They knew MSTY was always watching and assumed she would never overlook a reportable anomaly.

Kelly occasionally looked at the numbers when she needed a break from staring at the Manuals. She had mastered everything in the Manuals about the displays. Some were supposed to change, and others stay constant. A comprehensive understanding would require unraveling some exceedingly complex astrophysics and analytic geometry problems. Kelly was just beginning to grasp those disciplines.

∞∞∞

On 2 February 2034, Kelly was about to videocall Maureen once again to relieve her boredom. At that instant, she thought she saw out of the corner of her eye a change in the "perpendicular deviation" of Mirror 170. The display had never changed before, and now it was again fixed in a frozen state.

The change contradicted Kelly's understanding of perpendicular deviation. The Manual stated it was a fixed number, almost zero, that maximized the amount of sunlight reflected back into space.

Kelly's eyes widened. The change may only have amounted to a fraction of a percent, and maybe just for an instant. But why had it changed?

Kelly dictated a note to her electronic log, quickly recording her observations as the "2 February 2034 anomaly." Reviewing her note, Kelly couldn't remember if each digit was again the same as before, or if one or two were still different. She began to wonder if she had even seen a change.

MSTY didn't report anything about a change. MSTY's prime duty was to alert the SSPC humans who were ultimately responsible about any mirror motion that deviated from the Master Plan. It seemed peculiar that MSTY didn't flag the change, even if only tiny, that might need human attention.

Kelly knew MSTY had been monitoring the mirrors since NASA launched the first set about three years before. MSTY's powerful learning systems accumulated data and refined her monitoring algorithms far more quickly than any human could match. Kelly could never catch up with MSTY.

But Kelly reminded herself that MSTY was also learning on the job. MSTY had only a little more than 40 uneventful months of data to work with, and most of that time not all 480 mirrors were yet in orbit. The SSP Manual skipped over how the mirrors automatically adjusted to seasonal changes and the buffeting from the Sun and Earth's ever-changing radiation levels.

Still, something seemed wrong. The good news was that now Kelly had a real-life question to explore. Kelly quickly caught herself.

Slow down. Before I ring alarm bells, I need to dig into all the data and understand the relevant physics. But that will be more interesting than spending more time memorizing the damn Manuals. At least I'll understand more about what this one number means. Maybe I'll also learn more about how MSTY works.

Then, if I still have questions, I can raise the subject with my superior. Or maybe even Commander Fauré?

Chapter 3

Tourism Trouble

THREE YEARS EARLIER, IN 2030, Commander Fauré had begun meeting individually with the Directors to learn about their interests. He was particularly impressed by Director Mohamed Ibrahim's intelligence and extensive knowledge.

Ibrahim represented the World Bank on the SSPC Board. The Maldives Republic had given him a world-class education, which he repaid by pursuing a career in the Maldives' diplomatic corps. He had represented Maldives in UNESCO and the Association of Oceanic and Small Island States (known as AOSIS), and ultimately as its Ambassador to the UN and the US.

As a Vice-President of the World Bank promoting economic development in the twenty small island states that were slowly drowning in rising seas, Ibrahim had a deep interest in solar radiation management as a tool to mitigate climate disruption.

Beginning in the 2020s, climate disruption seemed to be tearing the world apart. Urban civilization was visibly deteriorating as expenses for "adaptation" overwhelmed government resources.

Widespread crop failures from droughts and floods meant inadequate food supplies for tens of millions of people. They abandoned their newly-barren farms and submerged coastlands in Central and South America, Central Africa, and low-lying regions in Bangladesh, China, Pakistan, India, Indonesia, and the Philippines.

These climate refugees pushed north and south into uplands and neighboring countries, with or without any governmental approval. Sympathy for refugees quickly morphed into self-protective national immigration policies. Those allowed to migrate to new countries were frequently destitute, lacking access to new farmlands or fisheries.

In September 2032, Ibrahim requested a follow-up meeting with Commander Fauré to discuss what he described as "certain problems with the SSP Master Plan." Commander Fauré quickly rearranged his schedule to accommodate his Board Member.

After the usual opening pleasantries, Ibrahim launched into a presentation about the impact of mirror shadows on communities that depend on tourism for their livelihood.

"I have reviewed the Master Plan thoroughly. While it's generally quite sound, it completely ignores the potential economic effect of mirror shadows falling on tourist resorts in small island states.

"Tourism is vital in these countries. Small farmers, fishers, local shops, and service industry workers depend on tourism to keep them above subsistence.

They are not well suited to life in modern urban environments and have no portable financial resources. The economic survival of this industry is their lifeline.

"As an SSPC Board member and the World Bank official responsible for the economic well-being of these countries, I feel obligated to ensure that the SSP does not add to their problems. The SSPC must address the issue of shadowing tourist destinations."

Commander Fauré listened thoughtfully, organizing his thoughts on this unexpected challenge.

"I appreciate your concern. We both know the kind of pressure we faced to get the mirror system into orbit quickly. Computer modeling inevitably determined the SSP mirror locations. We are already looking at various possibilities for adjusting them.

"Shortly after my arrival, I directed the Research Staff to initiate a Shadows Impact Study—an analysis of actual, measurable impacts of the mirror shadows on human, animal, and plant ecosystems affecting agriculture, forestry, fishing, and urban energy consumption.

"As you know, almost 70% of Earth's surface is deep ocean. Wind and ocean currents quickly disperse the solar energy arriving there. So the local impact will almost certainly be negligible.

"Some land impacts might be more significant. Now that NASA has launched all the mirrors, the Shadows Impact Study will collect valid ground truth about their effects. That data collection will take a few more years.

"We expect to conclude that the shadows have no significant effects on human, animal, and plant ecosystems, or agriculture, forestry, fishing, or urban energy consumption."

Ibrahim shook his head. Clearly, Commander Fauré didn't understand the urgent needs of the tourism business.

"I'm familiar with the Shadows Impact Study and its importance to add credibility to the net beneficial effects of the SSP for everyone on the planet.

"But you need to examine the tourist areas that are physically being shadowed immediately. Wealthy individuals and large organizations typically plan exotic vacations and conferences years in advance. Tourist facilities can't survive rumors for the next three or four winters that their forests, parks, and beaches will be gray rather than sunny.

"The Shield only needs to reflect a small percentage of the incoming sunlight, so you have a lot of flexibility. The results of your Shadows Impact Study are half a decade away, and then there will be controversy over adopting them. That won't do.

"I'm already hearing distress from facility operators. Doubts about adverse impacts from the shadows are undermining the scheduling of tropical destinations right now. The SSPC needs to counteract that threat."

Ibrahim's words made clear that this matter was not abstract, although he hadn't mentioned any specific locations. The Commander had no immediate answer, although he doubted that the effect would be noticeable anywhere.

"Are many locations affected?"

"I've only heard from generic concerns from the Tropical Tourism Association, so I don't know for sure."

Fauré paused.

Ibrahim is too wise to identify any place by name. If someone is rewarding him to raise this issue, that would be a conflict of interest, given his position on the Board. I can't ask, and I don't want to know. In any case, I must at least acknowledge the legitimacy of Ibrahim's concern.

"Let me look into the facts, my friend. Maybe I can issue a specific public statement that no known tropical tourist areas will be affected. I hope that would relieve these anxieties. If I learn that any mirror shadows would create serious problems for tourist destinations, I will do my best, within the rules, to address the matter."

"Thank you for that assurance, Commander. I doubt a statement would be enough, as I know some resorts are already hurting. Other tourist resorts have an interest in spreading this rumor, and without some certainty, all the tropical resort destinations will suffer.

"By the way, I have just taken a seat on the Board committee chaired by Director Malkovich to study SSPC administrative waste and mismanagement. The other committee members aren't paying much attention to its work. At this point, I don't think I would endorse any adverse conclusions."

The Commander immediately understood the import of Ibrahim's oblique reference.

His words suggest he'll take a helpful position but inevitably imply a threat to join Director Malkovich's attack if I don't address his tourism problem. I can't afford to have him join up with Malkovich and besmirch SSPC's reputation—and my own—for honest, efficient administration.

The Commander forced a smile and responded.

"My impression is the Malkovich committee is just a cosmetic device to attack the SSPC. He needs to show Moscow he's working to undermine us. I certainly hope you won't lend your knowledge and credibility to that effort. It would end the very program you have long supported.

"Let me look into what we already know on shadowing and how any adjustments could address any apparent problems. I'll be back in touch with you as soon as I know more."

"Thank you for your hospitality. I wish this matter were not so urgent. It's awkward for all of us, but the omission of tourism from the past studies was a serious error that the SSPC must remedy. I look forward to hearing what you learn."

With that, Ibrahim departed. Commander Fauré promptly asked MSTY for a set of maps showing details of the tropical coastal areas being shadowed. It didn't take long to identify the cause of Ibrahim's worries.

Most of the Maldives' vital resort hotels and tourist beaches would be under the calculated umbra or penumbra of Mirror 170 for several hours every day during the winter months.

MSTY concluded that people on the ground probably would not notice an uncomfortable difference in light levels, but that was not the point. Simply the plausible possibility of gray skies could be enough to divert conference and vacation plans elsewhere. Fauré sympathized with Ibrahim's concern.

He's naturally worried about businesses in his homeland. I need to fix this somehow, right away if I can. But I don't see how I can unilaterally announce some de minimis *adjustment to the alignment of Mirror 170 to protect the Maldives without even looking at impacts on other tropical tourist facilities.*

I'm not sure I have legal authority to deviate even slightly from the Master Plan without a public notice process and specific Board approval.

Even if I have the authority, that kind of response to implicit pressure will undermine the professionalism and scientific standing of the SSPC. It will inevitably generate similar requests from resorts in other island states who might be equally shadowed or affected by other mirrors. Acting to protect only one would raise awkward questions of favoritism.

I need to what I can do for Ibrahim without getting bogged down in lengthy, formal public procedures to amend the SSP Master Plan for the tourist industry.

Chapter 4

Threading The Needle

COMMANDER FAURÉ STUDIED every word of the relevant language of the SSPC Manuals, all of which he had personally approved years earlier. Under the standard procedures, adjustments to mirror positions first go through the Operations Staff and the Science Advisory Committee. Their recommendation comes to the Commander for his sign-off.

That would be just the beginning. SSPC decisions, like all UN and national government decisions, must be preceded by transparent public consultation. Any amendment to the SSP would require publication of an Official Notice stating the proposed change and its rationale.

The Notice would circulate to all UN Members and the global public for comment. The Commander could issue the final approval only after evaluating the public comments and the SSPC Board's views. The characteristics of this process would make it unsuitable for the matter at hand for several reasons:

- It would take time, many months or possibly years if the decision became controversial.
- The scientific community would oppose any "special deal" for any or all tropical tourism without a comprehensive review of the entire mirror system. Piecemeal adjustments would distort the original design, which optimized net benefits.
- Industrial groups will applaud this commonsense response to a technocratic oversight. Then they will ask for other, supposedly equivalent, changes of their own.
- Someone, perhaps even a Board Member, might claim the change was a corrupt favor. The media will hype the controversy and appearance of scandal.

Eventually, Fauré uncovered the technical and arguably legal mechanisms to make a slight adjustment to Mirror 170 in secret.

The technical solution is to send instructions directly to MSTY on my Emergency Terminal to make a series of minor adjustments to Mirror 170's perpendicular deviation. I'll direct her to put the records only in my personal, confidential files. No one else will have access to that information. I'll tell Ibrahim that the problem is quietly being solved.

My legal justification will rely on an exception built into the Operations Manual. Part 12.5.2 specifies that in "exigent circumstances," the Commander can directly send orders to MSTY to make adjustments in SSP operations "to avoid actual or potential injury" to human, animal, and plant ecosystems, or "affect agriculture, forestry, fishing, or urban energy consumption." The exception doesn't say anything about publicizing the action.

Part 12.5.2 does not explicitly mention "tourism," but that omission simply reflected a lack of imagination of the people who drafted it. The current situation certainly involved "potential injury" to human activity, and the delay would be damaging. Fauré would ask MSTY to verify adjusting Mirror 170's perpendicular deviation would not diminish the SSP's effectiveness in any significant way.

The concerns about legality, logic, and appearances remained. Refining the mirror positioning to minimize any unforeseen impacts of the shadows should logically await the complete Shadows Impact Study and public review.

Public notice of this "emergency action" might reasonably be implied from the rules. The media would inevitably call the action a "loophole" that prevented meaningful public input once they found out about the decision.

After weighing the alternatives and possible consequences for a few days, Fauré decided to proceed. The next evening, he turned on the single-purpose Emergency Monitor in his office and intended for communicating with MSTY in a crisis. He had never used the Emergency Terminal before. This exercise would be a valuable trial run for any future emergency.

Once signed in, he directed MSTY to make the necessary calculations and orally report her conclusions about the impact of realigning Mirror 170.

He was surprised to find MSTY raising questions about his inquiry. MSTY was developing her own sense of procedural regularity from reading the Manuals. She questioned the use of the Emergency Terminal for this purpose.

"Commander, you have never used this Emergency Terminal before, and you haven't explained why this use is appropriate. Are you requesting this information for your own purposes or for the SSP?"

"I am requesting it for the SSP. I need to understand the impact of a slight realignment of Mirror 170 on the Maldives tourist resorts and our other program objectives."

"But is this an emergency? Shouldn't your request and my response be recorded in the daily logs like every other inquiry and answer? I thought I should record and report everything the SSPC does."

Fauré answered unequivocally. "I haven't decided to do anything yet, and I won't until I have your answer. I may act by exercising my authority under Part 12.5.2 of the SSPC Operations Manual, or I may proceed differently. Please answer my question as soon as possible."

Once the Commander asserted his authority under the rules, MSTY complied. "Yes, sir, I understand. I will proceed with the analysis immediately."

MSTY took longer to conduct the analysis than the Commander had anticipated. Determining how much

Mirror 170 would need to move was quick and easy. But the impact of the repositioning on the overall SSP program depended on data and suppositions about the weather, climate, and economic activities of surrounding areas, as well as possible impacts on Mirror 170 itself.

Three days later, MSTY provided her conclusions:

"A minor adjustment in the Mirror 170's perpendicular deviation, say 0.20%, would move the shadow of Mirror 170 off the tourist resort locations in Maldives atolls. The reduction in the amount of sunlight reflected away from Earth after the adjustment would be so small that it will disappear, even when extended to five significant digits. The change would not show up in any of the analyses the SSPC regularly publishes."

Fauré's whole body relaxed with this confirmation.

"Thank you. Can you make this change in the perpendicular deviation incrementally over the coming 20 months, in pulses of 0.01%?"

"Yes. Slow, incremental adjustments would place less stress on the mirror."

"Excellent. Please begin these adjustments incrementally over the coming 20 months. Notify me if anything goes wrong.

"Place all records of our communications through this Emergency Terminal in my classified file. Give no one access without my specific authorization."

"Yes, Commander."

"Very good. Thank you."

Fauré breathed a sigh of relief.

Two weeks later, he met with Director Ibrahim, again in his office. Ibrahim was not dressed in his usual business attire and seemed to be spending the day as a tourist in New York. Fauré quickly reported his conclusions.

"Welcome. I have reviewed the shadow maps of Mirror 170 and obtained an analysis from MSTY on how realigning it might affect the achievement of the SSP's global mission. I'm happy to say that the small island tourist locations we discussed need not labor under the threat of any shadow from Mirror 170 in the northern hemisphere winter seasons. The existing alignment will change slowly over the coming months."

"Thank you, Commander. As you know, I have encouraged the World Bank to fund this kind of development, with some success. I think it is important that one branch of our patchwork global governing structure not undermine the effectiveness of other branches, notwithstanding their hypothetical legal independence."

Fauré nodded. "Since MSTY has determined that the realignment will have no impact on the SSP mission, I have not planned any public announcement at this time. I will include the change in the Master Plan general review when the results of the Shadows Impact Study are available."

"Very good. Thank you for your time and attention. I look forward to continuing to work with you in the years ahead. As far as I can see, you are doing an excellent job."

"For your information, the Malkovich Committee review of SSPC expenditures is going very slowly, and I'm not sure when, if ever, it will issue a report. But you can expect to provide an in-person defense of every major expenditure at some point."

Fauré smiled. "I appreciate that update. I will prepare accordingly."

"Thank you."

The Commander rose and walked Ibrahim to the door. He whispered to Ibrahim, "It is a pleasure to work with a practical Director like you. I hope you have time to enjoy the rest of your day in New York."

Fauré returned to his desk and took a deep breath.

Maybe now I can get a good night's sleep.

∞∞∞

After several months, Fauré had put the delicate matter of realigning Mirror 170 wholly out of his mind. MSTY made the monthly adjustments without difficulty, and no one except Ibrahim knew anything about them.

So far as he knew.

Part II

Chapter 5

Pursuing The Anomaly

KELLY'S RESEARCH INTO Mirror 170's position was a struggle. She needed to understand everything about the meaning and significance of "perpendicular deviation." She tried discussing it with Bill, who had a degree in spacecraft design.

Bill had a different agenda. "I'll review the Manual. Let's discuss the matter over dinner."

Kelly gave him a disdainful look. "I've already memorized everything in the Manual on the subject. I think I'll need to do some serious Internet research this evening. I'll let you know tomorrow if I learn anything new." Bill was disappointed by Kelly's response, but he got the message.

That evening Kelly learned the phrase was synonymous with the number of degrees (normally a small fraction of one degree) the mirror's vertical axis tilted away from the "perpendicular"—a line from the center of the mirror to the center of Earth. Keeping the mirror's axis perpendicular to Earth maximizes its shadow and energy production when the sun is directly overhead. Tilting the axis to make the mirrors perpendicular to the sun over the course of the day would reflect slightly more sunlight. But the constant changes in position would use more electricity and increase wear and tear on its fragile film. Every change in the mirror's position would require acceleration followed by deceleration, which would inevitably stress the mirror surface and supports.

The mirrors were already endangered by the growing quantity of space debris from disintegrating spacecraft. With no atmosphere to slow them down, the speed of the debris meant that objects as small as a millimeter in size would puncture the mirrors and create much larger holes. A fragment larger than several centimeters might destroy a whole mirror.

The mirrors individually completely blocked the solar disc in a circle about 30 miles in diameter (the umbra) and partially darkening a wider ring about 300 miles in diameter (the penumbra).

Despite diffraction and diffusion effects from Earth's atmosphere, the mirrors significantly reduced the sunlight's intensity and sharpness. That effect was the SSP's purpose—lowering the air, water, and soil temperature in its shadows and slowing climate disruption. Meanwhile, natural processes and new engineering technologies could reduce the atmospheric levels of carbon dioxide and methane.

Seasonal variations in Earth's orientation to the sun also shift the shadows' precise location, further reducing their total impact over any one point on Earth. The scientists' inevitably simplified models had roughly predicted the expected effects on the shadowed areas. The Shadows Impact Study would show the shadows' precise impact on human, animal, and plant activities. But the ground-truth data for the Study data was still years away.

∞∞∞

The unanswered questions in Kelly's mind about the change in Mirror 170's perpendicular deviation display were legion:

- *Was this minute change—only a tiny fraction of a percent—just an artifact of how the screen or sensors reported the number, a rounding adjustment of some sort—or a real-world event?*
- *If it did have real significance, what caused it? Should the mirror have been restored to its original position?*
- *Even if it was unimportant, why didn't MSTY flag it? Didn't it deserve documentation?*
- *Wasn't it MSTY's job to remember and report absolutely everything? Is MSTY truly following her instructions? Has someone changed them?*
- *If someone deliberately changed the mirror's perpendicular deviation, wouldn't that necessitate the Commander's approval?*

Kelly looked further back through the three years of data since Mirror 170 was launched in 2031. Fractional incremental adjustments in Mirror 170's perpendicular deviation appeared 14 times altogether, five of them since she arrived.

She was chagrined to realize she had missed those earlier changes. It suggested personal failures.

Flagging the anomalies now might expose the fact that I wasn't paying attention. But if MSTY didn't think these events were important enough to report, why would my error be important? Better to let the sleeping dog lie?

On reflection, she thought better of pretending she hadn't missed them.

I've gotten into trouble before by thinking I was smarter than everyone else. I'm in a much bigger, smarter world than I was at Casement. Making an error would be one thing; covering up an error would far more than double the offense. My job is to report what I saw if I think it's significant. If I am wrong, at worst I will look ignorant.

Kelly tried to imagine everything more the organization would want to know.

Is there a pattern to these events? Are they all going the same direction, or is the variation random? Did they always increase the perpendicular deviation? Was the mirror getting minutely further out of line?

A little extra effort on my part might help make up for my oversights. It would also show I can do more than just read the Manuals.

But the smart thing was to ask MSTY these questions. She reviewed MSTY's answers and cross-checked them against the readings of Mirror 170's other unchanging indicators. The essential facts seemed clear. Each of these pulses was real and had increased the mirror's perpendicular deviation in the same manner and direction.

So, Mirror 170 is now in a different position than it would have been without these changes. Various gravitational and frictional forces probably did not pull the mirror out of position, and the pulses weren't moving it back to where it belonged.

Did the pulses, individually or cumulatively, affect the functionality of Mirror 170? Perhaps MSTY concluded that these minor movements are of no consequence or even made them herself.

Conducting that analysis was far beyond Kelly's theoretical knowledge or computational ability. More questions for MSTY.

There's an important lesson here: just keep asking MSTY the right questions, and I will eventually learn what I need to know.

The next day, MSTY gave her the answers. After a day of study, Kelly was satisfied that she understood them—what they said and what they might imply. She finally felt ready to talk to anyone who would listen.

∞∞∞

Gaining direct access to the Commander would not be automatic, and perhaps even impossible, despite the relatively flat organizational structure of SSPC and his invitation at the Welcome meeting.

Kelly explained to her immediate supervisor that she had seen an anomaly in the information about Mirror 170 and thought it should be reported directly to the Commander. Her supervisor, whose sole focus was to prepare recruits for the induction exam, raised no objection to Kelly seeking a meeting. She knew Kelly would pass the exam.

The next hurdle was to get on the Commander's calendar. Jay Bhattachar was the gatekeeper. Nervous, she tried calling Maureen to talk things over with her. She got the voicemail.

I guess I'll have to sort this out on my own. I can't go on being the little sister forever. Anyway, what does she know about how things work in a military bureaucracy?

Kelly had only seen Sanjay briefly at the Welcome meeting, but he made a strong impression on her—tall, dark-skinned, large-boned, quiet, muscular, with a penetrating, intelligent gaze. His Indian background also intrigued her. On 2 March 2034 she initiated a videocall to him.

"Good morning, Officer Bhattachar. I'd like to talk with you about a problem I've run across. Is this a convenient time for you?"

Jay remembered meeting Kelly, one of the few female recruits. "Now's okay. Please call me Jay. What's on your mind?"

"As you know, recruits are supposed to keep track of the status of the mirrors whose data appears on the screens in our cubicles. I have tried to do so when not studying the Manuals for the Induction Exam.

"I recently observed a change in the perpendicular deviation of Mirror 170. I subsequently discovered several such changes had occurred. To my surprise,

MSTY did not report any of them. I think Commander Fauré should know about it."

Jay was inclined to be helpful. He hadn't previously run across anything about "perpendicular deviation" in his job. "I'll need to get the Commander's approval, but I can tell you the earliest open date is ten days away."

"Can't you squeeze me onto his calendar any earlier? This unreported change might reflect a problem with the Mirror or with MSTY, or both."

Jay simply repeated, "I'm sorry, but no videocall times are available before 1130 Friday, 10 March. I'll let you know what the Commander says."

"I guess that will have to do." She let her voice fall as she ended the conversation. Catching herself, she added, "Anyway, I appreciate your help."

Reflecting on the delay, Kelly was content with it.

I'm not even sure myself that the data or MSTY's analysis point to an emergency. The change in perpendicular deviation is tiny. It might just be an intentional act by MSTY, on her own or at the direction of some SSPC space wizard.

Another thought crossed Kelly's mind.

Perhaps the Commander himself made the changes! "Slow down, Kelly," Maureen would say. "You need to behave like a thoughtful adult, not a flighty, excitable newcomer. Perceptions matter."

You're still a recruit on probation. Ending up sidelined as an anonymous SSPC bureaucrat in New York could be worse than being a clerk at Casement. I want more than that. And I certainly don't want to wash out and go back home with no prospects at all.

Chapter 6

Kelly Talks With Fauré

THE NEXT MORNING, JAY raised Kelly's request with Commander Fauré.

"Kelly O'Rourke, one of the recruits, wants a videocall with you. She says she observed a change in the perpendicular deviation of Mirror 170, a value that the SSP Manual says is never supposed to change. MSTY didn't note it, and she thought you should know about it. I scheduled her for 10 March at 1130. Is that okay with you?"

Fauré looked distracted for a moment, then nodded.

"I can't imagine MSTY overlooking anything important. But I suppose it's a good practice to talk with a recruit who thinks she has learned something out of the ordinary. At least it shows she is serious about her work and wants to learn more. We should encourage that attitude. 1130 is a good time. I can cut it short if necessary."

"Yes, sir. I'll confirm the date and time with her."

Commander Fauré confidently assumed he could handle any recruit on any subject. He had studied aeronautical engineering in college and graduate school and entered the Force to be a pilot. He loved the physical sensations and adrenalin rush of risk in an airplane. Computerized, autonomous drones were ending all that.

Fauré's upward mobility now depended on his success as a bureaucrat. He concentrated on management skills and climbed the bureaucratic ladder through hard work, attention to detail, and sensitivity to the political needs and perspectives of colleagues and superiors.

He hoped success as SSPC Commander would be a steppingstone to command a UN Peacekeeping Force—a chance to exercise leadership and political skill in a situation where human judgment would matter.

Fauré kept his ambitions well hidden. His seemingly relaxed manner was calculated to induce a unifying sense of mission and camaraderie among the personnel from three dozen countries. Building the new SSPC into a cohesive team was a slow process that needed nurturing every day. Encouraging recruits was part of the job.

On 10 March 2034 at precisely 1130, Commander Robert Fauré appeared on Kelly's monitor in his crisp, silver-blue SSPC uniform. He looked every inch a Commander in Chief.

Videocalls had long replaced telephone calls in most professional settings, along with texts, photo and video sharing, and other quick communications.

Kelly was a bit flustered by the Commander's image and his salute, which she returned after a too-obvious pause. She could only see a small part of his office in the background. It seemed almost as bland as her cubicle—larger of course, but sparsely furnished with a simple desk and two chairs. No frills here. She could not see the spectacular view out his windows.

From Fauré's perspective, Kelly O'Rourke, a native of Ireland and a female officer in the Irish Air Force, brought precisely the kind of global representation and diversity to SSPC that he hoped to create.

Kelly's appearance—her bright red hair, fair skin, symmetrical facial structure, and slim shoulders—took Fauré by surprise. Her photos didn't do her justice. She was quite a change from the typical ex-pilots, engineers, and computer geeks SSPC among the recruits.

"Welcome to the Space Shield Project Command, Officer O'Rourke," he began, launching into his standard introductory speech. "I'm sorry we haven't yet had the opportunity to talk individually, and it's already been almost five months since you arrived! I hope you are enjoying New York City's unique attractions.

"We need more personnel with your academic credentials and willingness to work on this vital non-military project. It may not seem as exciting as preparing to interdict killer satellites. But the intellectual problems are just as challenging, and the fate of our planet depends on our success.

"What prompts your call?"

Kelly began her memorized explanation.

"Thank you, Commander. It is an honor to serve in your Command and be a part of its vital mission. I hope I can make a helpful and creative contribution to our work.

"I'll try to be concise. I work in the cubicle that contains the data displays showing the position and performance of Mirrors 160 to 179. A few weeks ago, I observed a tiny alteration in Mirror 170's perpendicular deviation display. The movement lasted for just a few seconds, after which the number was again static.

"I had not seen anything like that before—in fact, I was finding my windowless cubicle pretty boring. This unexplained change caught my eye because it did not seem to make any sense in terms of the Mirror's physics or mission, as I understand them from the Manuals.

"I expected a follow-up from MSTY, but she didn't issue any special report or alarm. Initially, I couldn't determine whether this short pulse was a real-world event, a statistical or sensor artifact, or a malfunction of the computer behind the display.

"Before bothering you, I took it upon myself to look through the accumulated data for earlier instances of this kind of pulse to Mirror 170's perpendicular deviation.

"I found 14 earlier occasions, each involving a tiny realignment of 0.01%. In response to my query, MSTY confirmed that each pulse did in fact increase the mirror's perpendicular deviation by that fractional amount. But she didn't issue reports on any of them at the time they occurred.

"I've been studying the SSPC and SSP Manuals and reading the UN documents on the creation of the SSP. I reviewed the Corp's decision logs and found no record of any relevant decision or even mention of these pulses or the resulting increased angle.

"As I read the Manuals, I would think such an adjustment would need your personal approval somehow. Perhaps you know all about this adjustment. If so, let me just leave you this Memorandum detailing my findings and analysis. I realize MSTY did not find this matter sufficiently serious to warrant any warning or report.

"If there is anything more I can or should do, please tell me. And thank you for your attention."

Commander Fauré glanced at the six-page Memo Kelly had electronically delivered as she talked. It included the data Kelly had painstakingly compiled and corroborated with MSTY.

Fauré's gaze turned stern. "Let me give you some history that you could not have learned from the official documents. The decision to create the SSP was intensely controversial. Governmental, scientific, and public interest organizations were and are deeply divided about its predecessor, the so-called tropospheric veil experiment.

"That experiment was an unauthorized scheme hatched by an unidentified handful of diplomats and governments—a low-budget, hastily designed effort secretly funded by one country and abetted by another. It would have been difficult to sustain, but it did demonstrate that a dozen drone aircraft continuously spreading calcium carbonate particles in the tropopause could create an atmospheric veil. The particles reduced the amount of solar energy reaching Earth by the fractional percentage necessary to slow the pace of global warming.

"It also unintentionally exposed the existence of a clashing Russian effort to hasten the breakup of the Arctic icecap, which would facilitate Russian shipping and mineral development in the Arctic Ocean. The discovery of these two conflicting secret and uncontrolled climate modification programs created a confrontation between the United States and Russia.

"The experiment ended when Russia shot down one of the drone flights, denounced it in the UN Security Council as an illegal invasion of Russian sovereignty, and demanded its termination. The US won the diplomatic struggle to create our program, but Russia has never forgiven the perpetrators.

"The UN Secretariat was tasked to recommend a solar shield plan. Instead of a veil, it proposed using reflective, energy-generating mirrors. The mirrors would have some value as an energy source even if they were ineffective in slowing climate disruption. This approach appealed to the defense industry, which saw profit opportunities in building this complicated, high-tech infrastructure.

"Many opponents argued that neither approach was safe, in part because any program would inevitably require trade-offs between winners and losers. They feared the powerful would be taken care of, regardless of what the scientists recommended as the optimal allocation of costs and benefits.

"We still have a long way to go to persuade the world that the SSP is fair and equitable. That is an essential part of our mission."

Commander Fauré paused to allow this flood of information to sink in. He did not praise her curiosity and diligence as she had hoped. Kelly said nothing, her face turning red as she absorbed his words.

He continued, "There is a lot more to learn about the realities of our mission than you will find in the documents. I commend your curiosity.

But for right now, please focus on your preparations for the SSPC induction examination. It may seem dull, but you certainly don't want to take the exam a second time. You aren't eligible for any other work here until you pass it.

"And please don't say anything to anyone about your conclusions or speculations on the meaning of the pulses."

Pausing again, he added, "Now I'm sorry, but I am late for a meeting with the member of our Governing Board from Russia. If you need more guidance, come see me again."

Commander Fauré saluted, and Kelly quickly returned the salute. Her screen went blank.

Kelly put her head in her hands.

Well, I guess he put me in my place. What should I make of his lecture and brusque departure? Maybe he was anxious about getting to lunch on time. Or maybe not.

Enough speculation. I need to bear down on memorizing the Manuals so I can ace the exam.

∞∞∞

Commander Fauré was equally concerned about the conversation with Officer O'Rourke, but for very different reasons.

If she found it, others might. O'Rourke herself might talk to someone about it. She's already said something to Jay. I need to find a way to neutralize this potential threat.

But right now, I need to focus on how to handle Director Malkovich and his phony expense records investigation. The O'Rourke matter will have to wait.

Chapter 7

Sparring Over Expenses

IMMEDIATELY AFTER HIS videocall with Kelly, Fauré called Jay into his office.

"I need to get to my lunch with Director Malkovich. Please take care of a couple of O'Rourke follow-ups as soon as you can. Send her Memorandum to Scientific Support to verify her observations, ideally by tomorrow morning. Ask MSTY if O'Rourke's Memo has fairly summarized MSTY's own analysis.

"And get me the full personnel file on O'Rourke. We can't afford to have some recruit send us on a wild goose chase just because she thinks she saw a couple of numbers flit across one of the monitoring screens. The Board of Directors would love to dip its fingers into something like that."

"Yes, sir. I'll get on it right away."

But "right away" didn't happen. The Commander walked into Jay's office two hours later and changed Jay's priorities.

"The lunch did not go well. Let me tell you a little more about Malkovich. He has been a UN Secretariat member working on international space programs and protecting Russia's interests for decades. Russia's support for the SSP has been grudging because its rogue predecessor had exposed Russia's secret, self-serving climate modification program.

"The UN had approved the SSP and the SSPC to manage it in 2027. Russia voted no, but the decision had been designated procedural and not subject to a veto. Russia did succeed in making the UN pursue the mirror system instead of a tropospheric veil. But it would still be happy to see it fail.

"The UN decisions explicitly bar the SSPC Board from exploring the wisdom of the SSP. So Malkovich is reduced to demonstrating vigorous oversight by poking around in our management expense records.

"He's trying to recruit Mohamed Ibrahim to join his attack. So we could be faced with two Board Members who are eager to pursue oversight of SSPC. Ibrahim is friendly to the SSP concept, but he has his own island-state ax to grind.

"Malkovich knows this probe into expenses is a charade, but he has to satisfy his superiors at home. Moscow could call him home and consign him to a make-work job or worse. He needs to show he's being tough. Most Board Members do not expect to find any wrongdoing. But I still need to defend my record.

"I'll need a set of display charts showing every significant expenditure in the travel and office equipment accounts before next Tuesday, 20 March. This effort takes precedence over everything else. I hope you can have a draft by 18 March."

"Yes, sir."

Jay found the assignment both tedious and demanding. He had to identify and summarize every travel and office equipment expenditure over *IMFEC (₣)* 5,000, place it on a free-standing chart, and justify it in less than 50 words—all that would fit in the physical space available. Paper versions of the charts would be circulated to Board Members, and they would inevitably appear in the media before long.

The explanation of every transaction needed to be accurate, transparent, and persuasive. Commander Fauré would rely on them to defend the SSPC's performance—and his own.

"For want of a nail, a shoe was lost; for want of a shoe; the horse was lost; for want of a horse, the King was lost." ran through Jay's head.

Why should the SSPC's whole future depend on whether some support staff person spent a few thousand extra ₣ on paper, or on computer cables that turned out not to be needed yet and were sitting in a closet for future use?

The answer is purely appearances. Malkovich needs to show he is policing the SSPC. And the media will eagerly jump on any item that would seem to the public unnecessary or too expensive.

It was not the work Jay imagined when he joined the SSPC.

On 18 March, he showed his draft charts to Commander Fauré, who requested several minor changes to make his answers more robust or concise.

Along the way, Jay had found a moment to call Personnel to ask for the Kelly O'Rourke file. Personnel replied that releasing the file to him would be a breach of the SSPC privacy policies. He would need to talk to the Personnel Manager for a waiver. He never had time to follow up.

He also asked MSTY to review the O'Rourke Memorandum. At least MSTY would respond promptly to his request while he was honing the charts.

∞∞∞

On 20 March, Commander Fauré and Jay appeared before the Malkovich Committee. Director Malkovich opened with a lengthy, deadening sermon about the importance of efficiency and frugality in managing UN resources. He characterized the SSP as a questionable enterprise that might do more harm than good for Russia and dozens of other countries suffering from climate disruption.

"You've had these hundreds of mirrors in orbit for four years now, and I don't see any real improvement in the climate they are supposed to transform. When will we have enough data to demonstrate that this project is a failure? How much money have you wasted so far? Why should we throw good money after bad to implement a remedy that isn't remedying anything?"

Commander Fauré's response aimed to lower the temperature of Malkovich's rhetoric.

"Thank you, Mr. Chairman, for the opportunity to discuss the operations of SSPC with your committee. I think you know the complete mirror system has only been operating for two years. We already know that it produces and distributes enough electricity to allow the worldwide shutdown of coal-fired powerplants. That change is significantly reducing carbon dioxide emissions.

"At least three or more years will be necessary to demonstrate with scientific reliability whether the whole system is accomplishing its climate mission. The SSPC has begun collecting and evaluating the data to understand its impact using facts, not mathematical models. We have nothing to say at this point on that subject. In any case, the wisdom of the mirror system is not within the jurisdiction of this committee."

Malkovich grimaced. "It most certainly is in our jurisdiction to root out waste and mismanagement at every level of this organization. So let's get into your expenditures, many of which need explanation."

Then Malkovich and the Commander worked through the list of Malkovich's 43 questions. Each question challenged an expenditure as too soon or too late, unnecessarily large or entirely unnecessary, or misdirected to a high-cost Western supplier rather than a less expensive Russian or South Asian supplier of equal quality.

Everyone's attention for the next three hours focused on Jay's charts. Of course, Malkovich was never satisfied. No other Director had said anything.

Finally, Director Ibrahim spoke.

"I have listened carefully to the questions and answers presented today. While a penetrating investigation of public expenditures is always appropriate, I don't think anything we see here constitutes a basis for criticism, let alone charges of misconduct. Building a new organization while at the same time managing the mirror operations is a daunting task.

"I want to commend Commander Fauré. Sir, you have handled the effort far better than we had any reason to expect. Please keep up the good work of maximizing the Solar Shield's benefits while minimizing its adverse effects."

No other member of the Committee spoke. Malkovich adjourned the meeting.

Fauré and Jay returned to the office, both exhausted by the ordeal. The Commander was more than satisfied with the result.

"Jay, your charts were invaluable and right on point. We had an answer for every question and nothing to apologize for. That's exactly why I brought you here."

"Thank you, sir. You handled Malkovich beautifully, sidelining arguments about the wisdom of the SSP and showing that you've managed expenses very well. Everyone in the room seemed to agree with Director Ibrahim's remarks. It's a pleasure to see my work put to such good use."

"Can I reward you with dinner?"

"Not tonight, sir. Tonight I need to be home with David, and he'll be waiting at the door to hear about our day's adventure. He's excited about what we are doing, and he tells me his friends at school are impressed that his dad is doing things they see in the media."

"I hope you don't regret coming to New York with me. I'm sure it's been tough since your wife and young son went back to Canada. I went through a divorce several years ago, and although it was all amicable, it's still an unhappy memory."

"I appreciate your understanding, sir. Yes, it is painful, but what I am doing now is the most important work I have done in my life. And I love living in New York.

"Sally and I met in college in Vancouver, but she grew up in a Courtenay, a town of 25,000 on Vancouver Island where everyone knew everyone, and nothing ever seemed to change. In retrospect, I should have guessed she wouldn't like the competitiveness and intensity of any big city. It was hard to send Jim back to Canada with Sally while David stays here to finish high school, but I think it was the right decision."

"I'm glad you enjoy working here. You're making an important contribution, and I appreciate it."

∞∞∞

When Jay had departed, Fauré turned to stare out his office windows at the fantastic view from his windows. They faced east, providing morning sun and a spectacular evening prospect, even in March: the East River itself, with constant ship and ferryboat traffic, the Queensborough Bridge and Roosevelt Island off to the north, and the high-rise Queens and Brooklyn skylines across the way.

Usually the view calmed him, but not this time. His response to Malkovich's grilling was an unqualified success, and Ibrahim's closing comments might have shut the door on the whole inquiry.

But Officer O'Rourke's probing about Mirror 170 had resurrected the ghost of a far more significant threat. He leaned his head on the chair's headrest and closed his eyes.

What a mess. That pretty little Irish recruit has no idea what she has stumbled across. She could be my undoing if she chose. Exposure of my decision to help Ibrahim could serve as the excuse to fire me and upend the whole SSPC and SSP enterprise.

Chapter 8

A Drink At McFadden's

KELLY WAS DETERMINED to watch the Mirror 170 screen's perpendicular deviation more carefully after her conversation with the Commander. But two months later, she knew she had missed more pulses.

The numbers were slightly different again: the latitude and longitude never changed, but now the perpendicular deviation was 0.18%. When she had reviewed the data records to write her Memorandum, the deviation was only 0.14%.

It seems to be a pattern. There's a 0.01% pulse increase every month since I first noted the change. If so, I missed the other changes. I never checked the cumulative change in deviation.

She was embarrassed. Despite her best efforts to keep watch, she had never herself seen any of the changes in the perpendicular deviation.

Some of the changes might have taken place on someone else's shift. The desk is covered 24/7, but I had only one of the two 12-hour shifts. But is it likely that all of them occurred when I was off? Some pilot I would have made. Daydreaming about some guy, I'd probably be dead by now—"pilot error."

Kelly also fretted that the Commander was not taking her seriously. He said nothing about the substance. He just ordered her, nicely, to say nothing to anyone about this matter.

He didn't say I couldn't look deeper into this matter myself. Kelly expanded her data search. To her surprise, she found data showing similar pulses to Mirrors 210, 220, and 226. MSTY hadn't reported any of them.

So maybe I should. But I can't tell my immediate supervisor. I guess the only open avenue is to ask Jay for another conversation with the Commander. In the process, I'll tell Jay the results of my research.

This conversation calls for an in-person chat over a drink. Maybe I can persuade Jay to talk; he's not like the typical guy I've met bars.

Later that afternoon, she videocalled Jay.

"Hi. Do you have time to meet after work this afternoon? I want to follow up on my Memo. I've found some additional information that puts the data I gave you in a new perspective. How does your calendar look?"

Jay hesitated. "I need to be home for dinner tonight with my son David. I can probably meet Thursday. I assume you know the rules about fraternizing among officers."

"Of course, I understand. This chat isn't that kind of meeting. I'm just trying to navigate an awkward situation, and I need your insight. Suppose we meet at

1600 Thursday so you can leave for home at a reasonable time."

"That should be fine. Do you have someplace in mind?"

"I like McFadden's Saloon on 2nd Avenue, just north of 42nd. It's a little Irish pub that's been around forever. Only about four blocks from here and only a few blocks from my apartment. Do you prefer someplace else?"

"The only restaurant I know around here is the Palm II, and it's too expensive. I'm happy to try McFadden's. See you at 1600."

Kelly arrived early Thursday afternoon and chose a quiet corner booth. When Jay arrived, they ordered drinks through the voice-activated automated service—she an Irish coffee, he a Guinness. The robotic bartender prepared and delivered the drinks.

The area behind the bar was a throwback, with dark wood paneling and substantial booth dividers left over from the days of the pandemic, away from the sports on the TVs and the noisy regulars.

"I have a couple of things on my mind. First, I find it unsettling that I haven't heard anything from anyone about my memo. The Commander told me not to talk with anyone about what I found. I don't have any idea whether he found it useful or just trash. Does the Commander usually respond to memos?"

"A memo like yours? I don't know. I don't remember him ever receiving a Memo he didn't request, and then he often discusses them in a meeting. There's no written response."

"I assume he entrusted you to read mine. Maybe you are still working on it. Or maybe I shouldn't even expect a response ever. If you have any insight, I'd welcome it."

"Not really. I'll only draft a reply if he asks me to."

"Then I'd like another videocall. But I don't know if that's appropriate in terms of how the Commander does business. I don't want to annoy him. You know far more about him and how things are done around here than I do."

"I can try, but he rarely meets with recruits who haven't passed the exam yet, unless they are in trouble."

Kelly paused to take a sip of her coffee.

"I'd also like to tell you what I've learned since I wrote the Memo.

Jay weighed his options. If there was more, he wanted to know what it was, and he didn't want to disappoint Kelly. But he couldn't tell her anything.

"Why don't you tell me what you have learned. Then maybe I can give you a better answer."

Kelly summarized her new data about Mirror 170 and what she had found about Mirrors 210, 220, and 226. Because they were in a public place, she only referred to the numbers, never using the word "mirror."

"The pulses reoriented all four. The movements are all minuscule, but they have all been permanently moved. There were no alarms, no reports from MSTY, and no explanation for the change in position.

"It looks like a conscious action, and I can't imagine how anyone except the Commander could have moved anything without a public record.

"Am I barking up the wrong tree? Should I just go back into my cubicle and wait, like a good recruit?"

Realizing her last remark was a bit too cheeky, she quickly added, "Sorry. Patience isn't my strong suit."

Jay's usually impassive face poorly hid his shock. He had also thought about whether the Commander was the source of these actions. He redirected the conversation.

"This new information is interesting, but I don't know whether it would matter very much to the Commander. Either the pulses and non-reporting are appropriate, or they aren't, regardless of how frequently they occurred or how much change they made, or how many mirrors were affected.

"I'll ask the Commander whether he's interested in talking with you about your new findings and remind him it would be gracious to respond to your Memorandum."

Kelly smiled warmly and immediately changed the topic. "Thank you. So, do you need to get home right away? I confess it hadn't occurred to me you might have a son. You're always in the office, so far as I can tell."

Jay followed her conversational lead with relief.

"I have two sons: David, who is here with me, finishing high school and preparing for college, and Jim, who is in Year 8 in Canada, living with his mother on Vancouver Island.

"They initially joined me in New York, but the City was just too much for Sally, who grew up thinking of Vancouver as a big city. She complained she never saw me and rarely saw the boys. When it became evident that my move here was permanent, we formally separated and divorced six months later."

"How did you feel about leaving India for Vancouver as a child? It must have been quite a change."

"Yes, it was. My ancestors were all military men. After Indian independence in 1947, my grandfather directed his organizational skills to growing and processing tea in Assam. His business success allowed the next generation to become successful academics in philosophy, literature, and mathematics.

"My father moved us to Vancouver in 2005 to teach English-language Indian literature at the University of British Columbia. It was a drastic cultural change for me, but I liked Vancouver.

"While still in high school, I took full advantage of the University's policy of tuition-free education for faculty dependents. I studied physics, astronomy, Hindi, Russian, and Chinese and earned my B.S. degree in 2021.

"Following the family's military tradition, I joined the Canadian Air Force and qualified as a fighter pilot. Physical pilots became obsolete when autonomous drones came into operation. The path to promotion meant getting into administration.

"In 2026 Commander Fauré, a rising star in the Canadian Air Force, selected me as his aide. When he was tapped to serve as Commander of the new SSPC in 2029, he invited me to join him. I jumped at the chance."

Forty-five minutes later, with Kelly's occasional prompting, Jay was still talking about his life, obviously enjoying Kelly's undivided attention. Suddenly, he looked at his watch.

"It's past time to leave. This was a pleasant break from the office. I'll let you know what the Commander thinks, and perhaps we can talk more then."

Jay gave Kelly ₣20 to cover his drink and tip and rushed out of the restaurant.

Kelly remained, ordering dinner for herself and paying the bill. She was pleased as she reviewed the evening's conversation.

I think I have just made a valuable friend. And my Mirror research isn't over yet. Maybe I can figure out what's going on here.

She smiled to herself. She had no idea what she might find, but she was looking forward to the challenge.

'Crack Investigator Kelly O'Rourke is on the case!'

∞∞∞

Ten days later, Kelly hadn't heard anything from the Commander or Jay. She wondered if she would ever learn more from anyone about the realignment of the Mirrors.

Maybe I can get Jay to tell me more. He's deeply devoted to David, but I can see he's overstressed and lonely. I still need him to set up another conversation with the Commander.

I'd love to put the Commander on the spot—show him that someone has changed the perpendicular deviation of several mirrors. He must already know.

Besides, I've had enough of my tiny cubicle, memorizing every line of both Manuals. There has to be a challenging job for me once I pass the exam. And I want it.

Kelly waited another week. Her patience ran out. She straightened her uniform, checked her makeup, and initiated a videocall to Jay.

"Hello! Just thought I'd check in to see if anything has happened with my Memo or the subsequent research."

"Not really. I've had only a few brief meetings with the Commander since we talked last. I reported your concern that you hadn't heard from anyone. I'm not sure he really heard me.

"He's been distracted and tied up every minute lately. I don't even know what he's worrying about."

Kelly responded gently. "Thank you for the update. I was going to suggest another meeting, but if you think that's premature, we can wait for another time."

"I'm okay with meeting again. Let's make it two weeks from now. I'll probably have met with the Commander by then, and maybe I'll have more to report."

"How about a week from Thursday? I still have other questions for you about potential career paths in the SSPC. And I always welcome an excuse to have an Irish coffee at McFadden's. Maybe you can come a little earlier, so you don't need to watch the clock so carefully."

"Okay. Let's say 1500. I won't need to rush home. My son is spending spring break with his mother and my parents in Vancouver. Of course, everything is always contingent on the Commander's demands."

Jay immediately regretted those words. *I should never have volunteered that my son would be away. I need to keep this strictly business. And now I have no personal excuse for leaving early!*

Kelly did her best to suppress any hint of her pleasure at this knowledge. "Of course, the Commander always comes first. Hope to see you then. Have a good day."

"You too." Pleasant images of talking with Kelly at McFadden's continued to float up from Jay's subconscious for the rest of the day.

∞∞∞

Kelly again arrived at McFadden's early and tried to relax over her Irish coffee while waiting.

Don't get too enthusiastic. A closer relationship needs to be his idea, not mine. If nothing happens this time, that's okay. It can come later. Or not.

Jay arrived on the dot of 1500.

"I'm sorry to say I haven't discussed your new research with the Commander."

Kelly's disappointment was evident, but her words said something else. "That's okay. It's not urgent; I'm just curious about what he thinks."

"I know. I'll raise it when I have the opportunity."

"Okay. I'm also curious to know more about the Commander."

"So far as I know, he's a complete straight arrow. He's been married and divorced, with no children. He currently seems to have neither interest nor time to look for a new female companion. I think he sees this job as providing the visibility he needs to break into higher ranks, and he is determined not to miss the chance. I suspect he's focused his ambitions on a senior command position in the Canadian Air Force or the UN.

"He's never led a military force in the field, which is a crucial credential for most military people. Heading a UN Peacekeeping Force would be a great step if the opportunity arose. But those positions arise unpredictably and infrequently. I don't know if his management experience here can qualify him, even if everything goes perfectly."

They sent in their dinner orders: McFadden's mushroom onion Impossible Burgers with French fries. As they ate, Kelly led Jay to talk more about David and his divorce. She also shared some carefully selected tidbits about her past, painting herself as an experienced but not loose woman. She elided the year experimenting in Europe and offered nothing about her failure as a pilot trainee.

Jay didn't press for more, afraid he would seem too curious about her past.

Kelly turned to her concerns about the future beyond her cubicle.

"I'll be taking the induction exam soon. I've memorized most of both Manuals. If I do well, what positions are likely to be open to me? I'm not here just to draw a military salary and live in New York. I need a professional challenge, or I'll be as unhappy here as I was at Casement.

"I think you know I earned my college degree with honors in aeronautical engineering. I also went through the full military training program for the Irish Air Force, including self-defense, weapons use and safety, and crawling under barbed wire with live fire overhead."

"Really! Well, I hope you never need your live-fire experience here. But several possibilities would test your creative ability and perseverance. Then, if you continue to do well, leadership roles could open up."

Jay briefly described the likely options for top-ranked new officers, indicating which ones would be most challenging and likely to lead to eventual promotion.

As the meal came to an end, Kelly thanked Jay profusely. "Thank you for spending more time with me. Your insights about SSPC are valuable to me. I've been pretty much at sea about what really matters here and what my options are.

"I hope we can talk more soon. I live near here, so let me know what fits your schedule. I'm almost always available for a drink on short notice."

Jay called Kelly for dinner three weeks later, when his son was again visiting a classmate overnight. He had news to share.

"I finally had the chance to talk to the Commander about your discovery about 170. I didn't say anything about the other ones. He seemed to take it in stride. He asked me to confirm with MSTY. Later I told him MSTY reported that your Memorandum was correct. He just told me to keep the information confidential.

"By the way, I told him I was impressed with your determination to dig deeper and your creative approach to the subject. If you write a Memorandum with your new data, maybe I can get it to him."

Putting her hand on his arm, Kelly replied, "That's very satisfying news. I appreciate your efforts. I don't see any way I can reciprocate, but if there is ever anything, I'll do whatever I can."

Jay could feel his face turning red. He hoped it didn't show through his dark skin in the low light. Retrieving his business composure, he replied, "I've enjoyed our conversations. Being the Commander's Executive Assistant is demanding and often frustrating, so just talking to someone who understands what I do is therapeutic."

Kelly smiled and leaned toward Jay. "Having a real human conversation in a leisurely manner over dinner is a special pleasure for me too. Your life is much more complicated than mine, but being a recruit has its own stresses."

Jay felt the need to escape. Kelly's touch was more powerful than he anticipated. At the end of the evening, Kelly gave Jay a casual hug as she thanked him for his kind words to the Commander. Jay felt a long-dormant sense of emotional and physical desire.

Chapter 9

More Dinners

JAY CALLED KELLY FOR another McFadden's Saloon dinner a few weeks later. Kelly found him more impressive and attractive as she learned about his considerate handling of his complicated personal life and tales of his grandfather's exotic military adventures.

Toward the end of the evening, she took a gamble.

"Personnel notified me yesterday that I not only passed the induction exam, I scored near the top of the class. I'd like to celebrate. I can make you a much better dinner than the manufactured stuff we get at McFadden's."

Jay said nothing specific in response, and Kelly let the matter rest. Jay texted a week later to set a date for dinner, and Kelly responded with enthusiasm. Neither said anything about where. Kelly waited until a few hours before dinner to send him a text with her address.

It was a bright April day, with trees in blossom everywhere. Kelly came home early to prepare dinner and opened the windows of her apartment. She changed out of her uniform and slipped into a striking sea-green sheath. Set the table for two. Adjusted her makeup to suit the lighting and added a touch of perfume. Decided against candles—too obvious and clichéd.

He arrived on time, with a bottle of Chianti. She took his arm at the door and offered a glass of Prosecco. The dinner menu was light and elegant—pan-fried halibut in a lemon sauce, carrots and parsnips with Indian spices whose aroma filled the apartment, and berries with whipped cream for dessert.

The evening's conversation was a lively celebration of Kelly's transition from recruit to SSPC officer. It wasn't long before the guardrails fell. She led him to her sparely decorated bedroom. They made love hungrily in the enveloping darkness, more than once. He was bewitched by her appearance, her tenderness, and her patient and skillful lovemaking. Eventually, he reluctantly dressed, gave her a passionate embrace and kiss at the door, and departed.

Kelly was more than just physically satisfied; she felt emotionally alive. The kitchen could wait for another time. Collapsing on the bed, she luxuriated in happy memories of his supple skin, his powerful arms and legs, and his ropelike black hair.

Using Jay for career advancement was no longer on her mind. More than anything, she wanted the pleasure of more days and nights like this one. She couldn't contain herself. She had to talk to Maureen.

"Hi, sis. Have you got a minute to talk? I've got important news."

"I'm waiting to pick up the kids from school, but I can talk until they get out, about five minutes from now."

"Okay, I'll give you the condensed version. First, I not only passed the induction exam; I had a perfect score. It was only a matter of memorizing the two program manuals, and I learned how to do that at St. Agnes School. So now I should get one of the top positions open to recruits, with real possibilities for promotion down the road."

"That's terrific! It sounds like you've made it in the big city. I was worried that the competition would be overwhelming, but you've shown them you're the best of the best. Dad will be very proud and no longer so worried about what will become of you in New York. Congratulations!"

"I've got other news as well. I'm in love with a senior officer here. His name is Sanjay Bhattachar, Indian, but from Canada. He's a wonderful man and a worthy human being. There are complications, of course, because he works for the Commander, but I'll find a way to take care of that. Please don't say anything to Dad or the others yet."

Maureen was more distressed than pleased.

"Kelly, dear, haven't we been down this road before? I thought you were past the one-night stands and flings. You just met him, and now you're in love? Please be careful!"

"This one isn't like that. Jay's not taking advantage of me. In fact, I'm sure he's afraid I might try to take advantage of him. He's older. He's divorced and has two boys. One lives with him, the other lives with their mother near Vancouver.

"Maureen, this is the real thing. I know I could happily spend my life with him, taking care of him. And that's what I want."

"Sweetheart, I've got to go. The kids are here. But please call me again soon. We need to talk more about this romance. Please don't do anything rash. I don't want you hurt in your moment of triumph!"

∞∞∞

The next morning Jay was a wreck. Commander Fauré noted his disheveled physical appearance and distracted mental state. "Are you okay this morning? You could take a day off, you know. You have been working pretty hard lately, and you have plenty of unused vacation time."

"Thank you, Commander. I'll be fine after my coffee sinks in. I just didn't sleep very well last night. My son was away overnight with a friend, and I'm not very disciplined about following the evening routines when I'm alone."

Jay's mind whirled.

The brief liaison seems unlikely to be discovered. David didn't expect a phone call last evening, and he hadn't called on his own. No one knew I was not home alone or having a drink somewhere—except Kelly, of course.

Jay had enjoyed the evening—every bit of it—too much to put it aside. He knew he would want more and would have difficulty not seeing Kelly when the next opportunity arose.

But he'd seen too often what happened when officers found themselves in continuing relationships that violated the unwritten code against fraternization.

One way or another, I'm personally vulnerable to Kelly's demands, which might quickly become whimsical or irrational. Am I sure enough about her integrity to risk her compromising me?

He recalled a quotation from Congreve, frequently repeated by his favorite college English teacher: "Heaven has no rage like love to hatred turned, nor Hell a fury like a woman scorned."

I cannot let this happen—it's too much vulnerability to a person I don't know well enough. There are so many ways she could hurt me, even if they would be self-destructive for her.

Determined to quell his agony and foreclose future temptation, he sent Kelly a brief text:

"We made a mistake yesterday. It won't happen again, but I will never forget it. Thank you."

Kelly was crushed. She had enjoyed Jay far more than she expected. Her hopes that Jay could provide her an inside track to advancement were only a secondary concern. And his text seemed to imply he reciprocated her feelings.

I didn't anticipate such self-discipline. Now he'll bend over backward to avoid any appearance of favoritism, just in case.

I'm not going to give up that easily. I want more than a one-night fling, a stepping-stone, or an occasional physical relationship. He's too valuable for that. But I can't be demanding or threatening—that's just what he fears.

"It didn't feel at all like a mistake to me," she texted back. "I'm eager to talk with you again."

After four days of silence, it was clear Jay would not answer her. Kelly steeled herself to be silent in return.

I need to step back and show some patience. I can hope I've hooked this fighting fish, but pull too hard and I'll snap the line.

She received no further communication over the next ten days. Unable to stand the silence, she sent him another text.

"Please join me for a drink at McFadden's tomorrow. I'll be there at 1700. Come whenever you can make it." She hoped she had chosen a day when David might have other plans. She received no reply but went to McFadden's at 1700 anyway. Bracing herself for a lonely evening, she sat in "their" booth nursing her Irish coffee.

Jay walked in at 1730.

Kelly smiled but maintained an appropriate distance as he sat down at her table. He ordered a Guinness and an Impossible Burger. She followed his lead. Sitting so close, she ached to touch his skin, his face, his hair.

Come on, Kelly, now you need to show some discipline. Jay needs to know that I can control myself, that he's safe and in control. And that I accept that fact.

She forced herself to remain frozen in her place. After some small talk, she asked if the Commander had said anything more about her memorandum.

Jay's response wasn't encouraging. "I didn't want him to know you told me anything about your new research, so I only asked him if I should send you a thank-you note. He said, 'Just let it go.'"

Kelly had received an excellent assignment after scoring first on the induction exam. But she was afraid to mention it to Jay. Saying "thank you" could imply she thought he had intervened—precisely what he wished to avoid.

The conversation turned to office chatter, how David was doing in school, and what colleges interested him. The discussion was warm and personal, but shortly after Jay finished eating, he paid the bill, said goodbye, and walked out of the restaurant.

Kelly ordered another Irish coffee, drank it alone, and slowly walked to her empty apartment.

So, where am I now? Will he ever show up again, or was that goodbye? Do I even have a friend now?

How can I call Maureen after I told her how happily in love I was a week ago? I certainly won't sound like a mature adult. I hope she hasn't told Dad or anyone else!

Anyway, I still have work to do to learn my new job. And I am going to dig deeper into the mirror mystery. Why would anyone want these specific mirrors moved? Did the Commander move them surreptitiously, and why would he? How and why would anyone else?

Chapter 10

MSTY Gets Cryptic

JAY FINALLY BEGAN ON THE two tasks he had pushed aside to work on the Malkovich preparations: collect and review Officer Kelly O'Rourke's personnel file, and examine MSTY's comments on her Memorandum.

Getting the personnel file was no problem once Jay explained to the Human Relations Manager he was asking for the Commander. The Manager fully understood the importance of keeping on good terms with the Commander.

The HR Manager had two real jobs: making sure his staff was responsive to all SSPC Personnel inquiries; and finding ways to hire the people the Commander wanted and reject, reassign, or fire the people he didn't. The personnel rules were so arcane it took years of on-the-job experience to know how to use their mechanisms to accomplish those ends.

So Jay's request was easy. The Commander had special authority to see any officer's personnel file. Jay was asking on the Commander's behalf, so the file was signed out to the Commander and given to Jay to deliver.

Jay reviewed Officer O'Rourke's personnel file, checked out her recent Facebook, Twitter, and Instagram postings, talked to the Irish Air Force Personnel Office, and looked at a couple of "personal profile" internet services to see if anything amiss appeared in her personal life.

The Irish Air Force had assured HR that the reason Kelly washed out of flight school was her inability to remain conscious when flying upside down and banking sharply. Jay had found it a struggle himself, though he managed to get through it.

The file did show multiple re-assignments in the months after the washout, which might suggest that O'Rourke was an uncooperative or unproductive worker. It showed no criminal record, no drug addiction, alcoholism, gambling, or other vices. She had not filed complaints about sexual harassment or gender or religious discrimination in pay or promotion. Nothing to see here.

Next, Jay plowed through MSTY's comments on Kelly's Memorandum. It was difficult. Jay was a flight engineer by training, and he had never specifically studied satellite design or operation.

MSTY identified more than two dozen "errors" in the Memorandum. Unfortunately, MSTY did not yet appreciate the significant difference between a minor grammatical error and a fundamental conceptual flaw that could vitiate the foundation of a paper's analysis. Jay needed to review and evaluate each error MSTY identified and flag any important ones for the Commander.

Several of the "errors" were about ambiguous sentence structure or syntax, which could mask more basic misunderstandings. Jay was forced to think carefully about what MSTY understood the sentence to say in standard English, whether Kelly's Irish English might have intended something different, and whether deeper issues lay below.

Finally, MSTY discussed data, statistics, sensors, the likelihood of a false positive, and the practical significance of a real change in the perpendicular deviation value. Some of this analysis was barely intelligible to Jay.

He stopped cold, however, when he read this sentence in MSTY's comments:

"I cannot explain to you how Mirror 170's perpendicular deviation was altered without any official record."

If MSTY cannot explain this omission, the whole SSP control system might be vulnerable. Even putting that possibility in writing could raise serious cybersecurity questions to anyone who reads it.

Did she choose the specific phrase "I cannot explain to you" why there is no official record? Is she being precise, or just not sufficiently skilled to see the multiple possible meanings?

Jay decided to discuss the matter with Commander Fauré in person before putting anything in writing.

∞∞∞

The next afternoon, Jay presented Commander Fauré a status report on the O'Rourke tasks.

"I've finished the O'Rourke tasks, but I need your guidance on a critical point before I put anything in writing.

"I reviewed her personnel file and took a cursory look at her current social media accounts. So far as I can see, she's clean as a whistle.

"She washed out of flight training because she lost consciousness when flying upside down or executing sharp banking turns. She argued for another chance, but her request was denied. She appealed for another chance but apparently didn't present any reason why another try would produce a different result. Then she spent six probably disappointed months at desk jobs. I think the Irish Air Force approved her request for assignment here as a chance for a fresh start."

Commander Fauré nodded as he accepted the files. "Good work. What about her Memorandum? Is it right?"

"Apparently so, sir. But I want to talk with you about it. MSTY confirmed that the pulses to Mirror 170 were multiple and real. But she didn't report anything in her system about the repositioning pulses.

"MSTY only says, 'I cannot explain to you why there is no official record.' That response suggests to me that someone hacked her system and ordered the changes after temporarily disabling the alert system to prevent the creation of any record."

Commander Fauré's eyes narrowed. "Go on."

"I didn't want to write this down for two reasons. First, I'm concerned that MSTY might have an unspecified cybersecurity vulnerability. Whatever the significance of the changes to Mirror 170, the hackers could probably make more fundamental changes if they wished. Credit card account thieves often make minuscule purchases to see if anyone notices, before trying more costly actions.

"Second, the repercussions if the public learns a hacker was able to manipulate a mirror could be explosive all by themselves. If a hacker can fiddle with our mirrors, they could damage or even destroy them, individually or all at once.

"Equally important, it would cast doubt on our ability to keep track of the mirrors. The SSP could end in a disastrous dispute over a management failure.

"You may want to seek out any cybersecurity keyhole and plug it without any reference to Officer O'Rourke's Memorandum. You might also want to direct MSTY to undo the changes to Mirror 170's perpendicular deviation."

Commander Fauré's face froze. "I see what you mean. It's a problem. I need to talk with IT about this matter. You needn't write anything more. I'll take it from here."

"Thank you, sir." Jay sensed the Commander was unhappy with his worries and quickly left the office.

∞∞∞

Commander Fauré was terrified by Jay's report.

Now Jay also wonders how someone could realign Mirror 170 without MSTY sounding an alarm or even making a record. Fortunately, MSTY didn't reveal what was in my classified file, even to Jay, so he suspects a hacker.

MSTY knows why she has no official journal record of moving Mirror 170. I'm sure she connected the O'Rourke Memo to the instructions in my confidential file. I could delete my files, but MSTY would raise awkward questions.

Commander Fauré called in Jerry Stephens, SSPC's IT Director. He responded explosively to the Commander's questions.

"It's impossible that anyone could hack MSTY! We've been testing against hackers from the moment we took possession of MSTY in 2029. We've tried every trick of the trade, including some new ones we invented ourselves, without successfully creating a keyhole.

"We have two techs working full-time on cybersecurity. MSTY has never even sounded an alarm about a potential hack attempt!"

Commander Fauré waved his hand dismissively. "Apparently MSTY doesn't think it's impossible. Why don't you ask her and see what she suggests as possible avenues for a hacker? Have your techs tried that? I have to think that MSTY wouldn't offer an explanation that she thought was impossible."

Stephens's face wrinkled in distress as his mind envisioned disaster.

Protecting MSTY from any possible hack is my most important responsibility. If after five years MSTY is still vulnerable, I am the inevitable fall guy. It would make no difference that nobody else could have done better. Where could I find another job if I'm dismissed for having failed at this one?

"I don't know if they've tried that, sir, but I'll get them on it right away. If a keyhole exists, I promise you we'll find it in short order. I'll report to you on our progress daily."

"Daily reports won't be necessary. I know you understand the seriousness of this matter. Just let me know when you find something. And keep it low-key.

"Most important, please make certain no one knows where the suggestion to look for keyholes this way came from, or that MSTY suggested she might have an undiscovered keyhole. Just treat it as another effort to test and protect our systems.

"That will be all. Thank you."

Stephens left the Commander's office without a word, more worried than when he arrived.

Commander Fauré knew he had taken a gamble.

If MSTY leads Stephens's people to me, it could threaten the entire SSPC and SSP. I need to think about how I would respond to Jerry.

Officer O'Rourke might also figure it out. I wonder if her record really is 'clean as a whistle,' as Jay said. Let's see what my buddy in Canadian Air Force Security can tell me about Miss O'Rourke.

Two weeks later, Fauré knew more about Kelly O'Rourke than she probably remembered herself—

youthful experimentation with cocaine and marijuana, casual beach party sex, a year wandering around Europe meeting men, and a significant, emotional breakup shortly before enlisting in the Irish Air Force. And details about when she started flight training and how long she flew before she failed the final test, and what it might imply.

Fauré wasn't surprised.

A woman as attractive as Kelly usually gets her choice of men for as long as she wants them. Sometimes her beauty can be a disadvantage because people assume there's nothing more there.

But there's more to Kelly than that. Now she's reached the age where she wants to be taken seriously, and she's intelligent and inquisitive. A woman like that can be a powerful force.

Fauré wasn't sure how he might use his new information about her past. But having it gave him some comfort.

At least I have a tool that might persuade her to be quiet if I need to bottle up what she learned.

Part III

Chapter 11

Searching For A Keyhole

WUHAN, CHINA'S NINTH-LARGEST city, is the capital of Hubei Province and was China's national capital twice in the 20th Century. Its location at the convergence of the Yangtse and Hanshui rivers made it a prime transportation and manufacturing center throughout human history. The city's new archeological museum beautifully displays the region's ancient, sophisticated culture.

Wuhan's global reputation as an ideal place to live still suffered from the suspicion that it was the source, rather than the victim, of the coronavirus pandemic of 2020-24.

Over a decade later, that unhappy episode was still associated with Wuhan in people's minds, worldwide and in China. The national and provincial governments worked to counteract this weakness by subsidizing new high-tech companies and defense installations to locate there.

The Master Computer Systems Center, which designed and evaluated the most advanced cybersecurity technologies for the Chinese Air & Space Command, had recently moved to Wuhan. It occupied a building on Huanshan South Road at the edge of the Wuhan University Campus.

In June of 2027, the Center recruited Zhang Xingwen, Cai Jin, and five others from China's top computer sciences programs to join its elite staff. They were young, ambitious, and talented, and their work taught them the most advanced cybersecurity techniques for protecting the Command's systems.

Within two years, they had become top=flight cybersecurity analysts. Private sector internet companies who needed the same skills began courting them. Two of the seven immediately accepted offers that offered an escape from Wuhan and at double their salaries.

Zhang Xingwen, the team leader, came from a rural working-class family that the pandemic had decimated. Unmarried, introverted, neither handsome nor charming, the team was his daily family. He was distressed to see it disintegrating.

He floated the idea that the five remaining team members find an employer who would take them all. They found a few prospects but no offers.

Cai Jin, the other team leader, was a hard-working, ambitious only child who grew up in Wuhan. She had the benefit of regular tutoring and excellent schools from childhood through college. When she showed an aptitude for mathematics and computers, her teachers encouraged that interest.

Her advanced work in cybersecurity surrounded her with bright, diligent, ambitious men attracted by her looks and style in clothing and jewelry. She married the man of her choice without revealing the extent of her family's wealth beyond what was evident from seeing their home. Jian, her husband, had found secure, satisfying employment as an administrator of computer systems in the Wuhan provincial courts.

Cai shared Zhang's desire to preserve the team and stay in Wuhan. She suggested a different approach to their dilemma.

"Why don't we organize ourselves as a private consulting firm, stay here in Wuhan where we are already settled in, and provide consulting services to the companies who need our expertise?"

Zhang was not in a secure position psychologically or financially to take this path. "I don't know if I can afford it. It's likely to be slim pickings for a few years even if we ultimately succeed."

"Yes, but in the long run, we'll be far better off financially than in government service and probably better off than being an employee of some high-tech business. I think my parents will help us get started."

Zhang trusted Cai's judgment, and he was afraid to lose her. "Okay, let's give it a try."

They set up Defense Incorporated (CDI) in July 2031 and rented office space on the ninth floor of the Dong Hu building on Huanshan South Road, a block from their former office, with a view of East Lake.

The last three team members—Yi Gong, Hua Luo Dan, and Wei Tong—were also hesitant to give up their secure military jobs. Besides higher social status as patriotic service, they assured early retirement at almost full salary. But they hoped to join CDI when it had enough work to afford them.

CDI's clientele quickly expanded. Within a year, they invited Yi, Hua, and Wei to join CDI as junior partners. Wei Tong chose instead to take a lucrative position with Tencent, one of China's largest internet gaming and marketing firms.

Zhang and Cai were happy to have preserved most of their original military crew. Their business continued to expand rapidly as their expertise became known. By 2033 the partners' net incomes were nearly double their military salaries.

∞∞∞

In January of 2034, another cybersecurity firm, Network Security Systems Incorporated (NSSI), approached CDI for help with cybersecurity defense for one of their clients. Jordan Milhous, NSSI's President, explained the project, codenamed "Greenhouse.

"We're already well underway, and we've found nothing. But we can't satisfy our client that no potential keyholes endanger their state-of-the-art computer system. They want a formal "second opinion" from CDI that no keyholes exist in the Greenhouse system."

Cai was enthusiastic. "It looks like an excellent opportunity for us to sharpen our skills at their expense."

The situation was unusual in two respects, however. First, the compensation would be purely on a time basis with no upper limit until CDI was itself satisfied that no keyholes existed. Trying to prove a negative is a consultant's gold mine – how do you know when you have succeeded in proving no keyhole exists? Of course, NSSI could call a halt to further work at any time.

Second, NSSI refused to reveal the name of its client, claiming disclosure would be unethical. Zhang surmised that NSSI didn't want to share the credit. "NSSI will want to claim credit for our work if we do find a keyhole, rather than admit it needed outside help. And we'll be unable to exploit the work as a marketing tool."

No precise industry-wide ethical principles or legal limitations existed in China on how cybersecurity firms should operate. But NSSI's proposal raised obvious ethical concerns. Cai raised the issue with the partners at the next team meeting.

"The only way to test an unknown computer system from the outside is to explore ways to break into that system. CDI will be relying solely on NSSI's assertion that the Greenhouse system's owner has authorized CDI's activities.

"Shouldn't we insist on meeting with someone from the owner of the Greenhouse system before we start messing with their computers?"

Zhang, unwilling to pass up this lucrative opportunity, argued vehemently for going forward.

"Look, we always work with agents who say they represent their clients, either as employees or consultants. How do we know any of them are genuinely representing their organization's interests rather than their own?

"If we say no to NSSI, we're not just cutting off this opportunity to show and build our capabilities. We're probably foregoing any future work from NSSI. We've staked our financial future on CDI's success. I don't think we can be so particular about our selection of clients."

After further heated discussion among the partners, Yi proposed a compromise.

"Let's ask Jordan for a meeting with a representative of the Greenhouse system. We'll see what he says. If we're satisfied with what we hear, we proceed; if not, we decline. Zhang and Cai must both be satisfied. This decision is important, but not as important as holding our team together."

Cai called Jordan.

"We're eager to do the work. But before we begin, we'd like to meet with a representative of the Greenhouse system's owner. We're not comfortable poking around in someone's system without their knowledge."

"That would breach our client's confidentiality," Jordan replied.

But Cai persisted, and he finally agreed to arrange a meeting. All four CDI partners attended the meeting. A tall, slim, dark-skinned man, about 40 years old and impeccably dressed, accompanied Jordan. He introduced Christopher Kangata.

"Everyone calls me Chris," he said, passing his credentials to the CDI representatives. His ID showed he was an employee in the SSPC IT Bureau. Chris explained why this work was so sensitive and essential to SSPC.

"Our computer systems must be foolproof. Interference with solar mirror operations could hurt many thousands, or maybe our entire planet.

"SSPC cannot allow someone to pervert our system into a mass destruction weapon, or even claim to. It could doom the whole project. Not everyone accepts solar geoengineering with mirrors is good. We must reassure everyone.

"We cannot say anything in writing. You will search for computer system flaws for NSSI – a subcontractor. If it goes well, NSSI will give a strong recommendation and bonus.

"If it becomes a public concern, we will release your Second Opinion to defend the reputation of SSPC. But that's our choice, not yours."

Chris's Kenyan speech rhythms and patterns were problematic for Zhang and Cai. Their Chinese English teachers never studied outside of China and never covered the vocabulary of complex business arrangements. Nor did they explain African or Indian English—people for whom English was also a second language.

Chris seemed to have as much trouble understanding Cai's and Zhang's questions as they had understanding his answers. They got the gist of what he was saying. But seeking detailed explanations to complex system design questions was unproductive.

Nevertheless, Zhang and Cai were satisfied with Chris's answers. They took the assignment and began working immediately, eager to test their skills against the prestigious new UN SSPC.

They didn't stop to examine other possibilities.

∞∞∞

After the meeting, Jordan and Chris stopped at a tea house not far from CDI to celebrate the successful conclusion of their effort to hire CDI. They believed that if CDI could find a keyhole, the ability to tap into the SSPC computer system would somehow generate attractive financial returns.

The two men had known each other since college. They quickly became soul mates, both growing up in the US as children of diplomats. Jordan's father had headed South Africa's Ministry of Trade in Washington. Chris's father was the Ambassador of Kenya to the UN. By the time of their graduation, shifts in political control in their countries had left both fathers scrambling for new employment amid the global financial collapse.

Without sympathetic connections at home, the usual jobs for diplomats' children—in international finance on Wall Street or at a leading national bank at home—were unavailable. They were on their own. The circumstances left them with less honest uses for their international contacts.

Jordan lauded Chris for his outstanding performance in the meeting with CDI.

"You gave a compelling explanation of the importance and urgency of finding and closing any keyholes into the SSPC system. Your convoluted English made it easy to evade the hard questions. The CDI folks are happy and eager to dig into the project. So now, some of the world's best computer wizards will be working feverishly to find an unknown pathway into the SSPC computer system. If they succeed, I'm sure that capability can bring us large rewards in many ways."

"Thank you. But I don't know if we should assume CDI and its staff are trustworthy the way they assume we are trustworthy. We need to track what they are learning and what they are doing with it. We won't have what we want if CDI decides not to give us their work or hatches mischievous plans of their own for it."

Jordan quickly recognized Chris was right. "Good point. We are still a long way from the finish line. Any ideas about how we can protect our investment?"

"Suppose we tell our team in Harlem to hack CDI's computers and monitor what they are doing? Maybe we could turn on their cameras and microphones and hear their conversations 24/7. Our guys may not be able to find a keyhole into MSTY, but they're probably good enough to hack CDI's computers. They're still a new business, and maybe they haven't done a disciplined analysis of their own system's weaknesses."

"That's a capital idea, Chris. Go for it."

In a month, NSSI's computer team hacked its way into CDI's system. Soon they had access to everything CDI was doing and saying.

∞∞∞

Cai assigned Hua to find a keyhole into MSTY, helping him out when he ran into brick walls. CDI was busy and being paid well for its efforts. After seven months, Hua felt he knew more about MSTY than the SSPC IT department.

Finally, Hua had an inspiration. He evaluated it, double-checked his work, and approached Cai, a little fearful that she would find a flaw in his thinking and dash his hopes for success.

"I think I've found something. Rooting around in the SSPC documents and files, I found the list of SSPC employee passwords. Access to MSTY from the SSPC computers requires electronic verification using facial recognition, which we can't duplicate.

"It crossed my mind that the Commander might have unique privileges, just as our military commander did. I combed the SSPC Operations Manual for some indication. It turns out he does. He has an Emergency Terminal, which is intended only for his use and only in extraordinary situations. It's located in his office. In addition to its secure location, it requires both the usual verification by facial recognition and a unique code that changes weekly.

"But the Commander can also reach MSTY with the code alone from an external computer, just as if he were at the Emergency Terminal. The designers gave the Commander the ability to reach MSTY from an Internet device anywhere in case of an emergency, even if that device didn't have facial recognition capabilities. I guess they thought the weekly change in the Commander's code would be sufficient protection from hackers.

"Now that I've hacked MSTY's operating files, I can get the code when she gives it to the Commander. I think I can pretend to be the Commander using the code alone. So we can tell MSTY to do whatever we want. She will assume it's the Commander because he is supposedly the only one with the code."

Cai smiled excitedly. "Good work, Hua. How can we take advantage of it?"

"We can set up a remote Emergency Terminal right here and demonstrate a keyhole that SSPC needs to fix. NSSI should give us a bonus for our success!

"The fact that we've found one keyhole doesn't mean there aren't others. I suggest you ask Yi to try to establish remote access to the Emergency Terminal while I continue to brainstorm other possible keyholes."

Cai praised Hua effusively. "Good thinking, and congratulations on making CDI a success! Let's adjourn for a dinner with the whole crew to celebrate your achievement."

Naturally a loner, Hua glowed with pride. He had distinguished himself as a vital member of the team after months of inconclusive and seemingly unproductive searching.

Chapter 12

CDI Finds Too Much

IN THE MORNING, YI BEGAN the task of remote access to the Emergency Terminal. In a few days, she demonstrated something well beyond Hua and Cai's original expectations.

"I've cloned a virtual Emergency Terminal here on my computer. We could give instructions to MSTY through this Emergency Terminal right from Wuhan."

"Before you do anything else," Cai suggested, "see if you can find out if the Commander has ever used the Emergency Terminal and why he used it. There must be a record somewhere."

Yi, pretending to be the Commander, asked MSTY to show her the Commander's calendar and all of his previous instructions to MSTY through the Emergency Terminal. MSTY asked Yi the same skeptical questions she had asked the Commander, but Yi had done her homework and knew how to respond. MSTY provided the information when Yi invoked the appropriate provisions of the SSC Operations Manual.

Combing through Fauré's calendar and noting the date of his one set of instructions to MSTY, Yi recognized a connection between the Mirror 170 adjustments and his meetings with Director Mohamed Ibrahim.

"Zhang! Cai! Come look at what I found," she practically shouted, showing them the Mirror 170 communications, the Commander's calendar, the relevant provisions of the SSP Operations Manual, and the exception the Commander had invoked.

Zhang and Cai looked at each other in shock. They immediately proceed to Cai's corner office. Her ornate furnishings calmed her spirit every time she took her eyes off her screen. The authentic antique furniture and decorative jade carvings were gifts from her parents to help her cope with the pressures of work. At this moment, she desperately needed the gentle Buddhist aura they exuded.

To avoid any possible electronic eavesdropping, Cai turned off her computer. Zhang's whole body was tense from the stress of the situation. He spoke with quick intensity.

"This information is more than we wanted. What should we do with it? It looks like the Commander is secretly realigning Mirror 170 at Ibrahim's request. If we were still in the Air Force and observed this behavior, we would report it to our superior or the Inspector General."

Cai was equally distressed and uncertain how to proceed. "We don't have any superior here; we're it. Our job was to find a keyhole, not catch the Commander doing a favor for a Board Member, if that's what it was. It's not our job to share this information, which is not within our scope of work, with anyone.

"Moreover, we have acted illegally ourselves. We took this information from a classified SSPC file without permission. The Commander specifically instructed MSTY not to include these actions in the publicly available SSPC records. We had no right to see it."

"I agree. But should we hide something that looks like favoritism and implies corruption?"

"I guess the right thing to do is talk to the Commander. He is, after all, our ultimate client. We can tell him that we found these entries while studying MSTY for SSPC as a subcontractor to NSSI. If he can explain why this action was in the interest of the SSPC, not illegal, and involved no personal benefit, that would be the end of it."

Zhang disagreed on that.

"We do have a superior. Our client is NSSI, not the SSPC. We are working for them, and it's up to them to decide what to do with what we found.

"I'm not sure we even need to tell NSSI what we discovered in the Commander's files. We can just show them the keyhole and explain how to fix it. That's what we are getting paid to do. It's their job to decide whether to look at the Commander's files. We're not policemen for the world. Anyway, how can you contact the Commander without violating our contract with NSSI?"

Cai frowned. "I'm not persuaded that we should tell anyone how to access classified SSPC files through the

Emergency Terminal. Let's give this more thought and make our decision tomorrow."

After dinner that evening, Cai excused herself from the usual family hour with Jian and their daughter Binbin. Their 120 square meter apartment was large and well-appointed for a young Chinese family. They could only afford it through a combination of assistance from Cai's parents and her own disciplined approach to consumer spending.

Cai hated leaving Binbin and Jian early. She loved every minute of their after-dinner hour. Binbin was growing up so fast! Now almost six, Binbin showed new layers of knowledge and skill every day.

Cai closed the beaded curtain door to the windowless cubbyhole that was Binbin's playroom during the day and Cai's office at night. She needed to think through the NSSI/SSPC matter. The more she thought about the situation, the more distressed she felt.

If we don't tell anyone, we'll be complicit by failing to expose this potential wrongdoing. In the military, it would be our duty to report anything we think is misconduct. Surely the same logic applies here.

But where would we report it? I suppose we could take this matter to the accounting or ethics officers in some UN internal oversight office. But I doubt that is how consultants in the private sector behave.

Another thought added to Cai's anxiety.

We never really tried to verify NSSI's connection to SSPC. We were so impressed by Chris that we took his credentials at face value. We didn't even make the most rudimentary check—is he listed as SSPC staff? We could have quickly done that.

Suppose NSSI isn't working for SSPC at all, but hired us to find a keyhole so they can hack MSTY? I'm sure NSSI find ways to use the keyhole to profit by illegally redirecting the SSP's resources.

And we could be prosecuted as accessories to their crime! We'd insist we knew nothing about NSSI's fraudulent intentions, but why would anyone believe us? We hadn't done any real due diligence!

I'll walk through all this with Zhang first thing tomorrow. We mustn't share this information with ANYONE except Commander Fauré.

The next morning, Cai and Zhang met again. "I gave this matter a lot of thought last evening," Cai began nervously.

"I think our situation is even more precarious than we realized. Look at it this way. Suppose NSSI uses our work to hack MSTY for criminal purposes. They might offer favors to countries or private interests that are unhappy about the actual or potential impact of the Solar Shield. Or they might disrupt the flow of electricity from the mirrors.

"If NSSI gets caught, they would claim CDI was the mastermind behind the hack. The media would spread the story far and wide.

Our denial wouldn't be very credible. We didn't thoroughly investigate or verify NSSI's background or Jordan's or Chris's credentials. How would we justify doing this work without investigating first? And shouldn't we have been suspicious when NSSI put us on an unlimited budget?

"We might not go to jail, but our questionable conduct would be the end of our business. We need to minimize these risks. So I still can't think of a better strategy than talking with Commander Fauré to see what he says."

Zhang hated the idea of going around their client. "What would that do for our reputation? We're a subcontractor, but we didn't report our results to our client. Instead, we went to their client and exposed our work directly. Isn't that a breach of ethics too?"

Cai dug in. The more she argued her position, the more she convinced herself. Zhang took a slow breath as he watched Cai get more entrenched.

We must stick together. But I don't want to lose our most lucrative client.

"I see what you're saying, and I recognize the risks of telling NSSI what we know. Honestly, I doubt you can reach Fauré just by saying you're a subcontractor to a contractor to the SSPC IT Department. I'll be amazed if you can even get to the IT Director, and you can't tell him anything."

Cai smiled. She had already thought about how to reach Commander Fauré.

"So, it's 'Bring me the broomstick of the Wicked Witch of the North.' Maybe it *is* an impossible task, but at least we can say we tried. If I only reach the IT Director, I could simply ask if he knows Christopher Kangata, who claims to be a member of his staff.

"We can decide what to do next after I talk to Fauré, or we give up on trying to reach him. I agree it's not our job to play detective or vigilante inspector general. But we need to know more before we do anything else. Today is 15 December 2034. I'll concede if I can't get a conversation with one or both by February 15."

I could ask MSTY to ask the Commander for permission to set up a call with a cybersecurity expert who needs to talk with him. I can give MSTY a general introduction to CDI as computer experts who have requested a conversation.

Cai meticulously combed through the SSPC Operations Manual and MSTY's conversations with Fauré that Yi had printed out. If MSTY once identified Cai as a hacker, she wouldn't get a second chance. She couldn't afford to make a mistake that would cause MSTY to lock her out. After mulling over various other options for a few days, Cai abandoned that approach.

I don't think that'll work. The Commander would immediately think it was a marketing call and refuse it. I need the Commander to wonder who I am.

Then she got a better idea.

I'll impersonate the Commander and send a message to MSTY to "schedule a call on my regular calendar" for a specific day and time. Then I will call him on the Emergency Terminal at that time.

Since only he and MSTY are supposed to have access to that computer, he'll instantly know that I've hacked MSTY. He will be outraged and hostile, but I'll have his attention.

I'll explain who CDI is and why we have been working on hacking MSTY. Then I'll ask a few questions about Chris Katanga and then about Mirror 170. I hope he will answer, and we can proceed from there.

On 10 January 2035, Cai, pretending she was the Commander, sent written instructions to MSTY to "add a call with Cai Jin of CDI to my calendar on 5 February 2035 at 1900."

MSTY objected to using the Emergency Terminal to put a routine meeting on the Commander's calendar. "Mundane matters like this should go into the open calendar that your staff, and eventually the world, will be able to see."

Cai mimicked the Commander's arguments in response. "This conversation is about a secret cybersecurity matter that I am exploring on an emergency basis. I am not ready for anyone to know about it yet."

MSTY deferred when the explanation for using the Emergency Terminal involved cybersecurity.

Chapter 13

NSSI Schemes

NSSI AUTOMATICALLY LEARNED about CDI's access to Commander Fauré's Emergency Terminal through their real-time computer surveillance of CDI. Chris Katanga assigned Yazeen Abdulla, a senior member of the NSSI staff, to monitor CDI's activities using its clone. Yazeen was a native of South Sudan, but he had volunteered and fought for ISIS in Iraq for a few years in the 2000s. He eventually defected to the US forces and told all he knew about ISIS.

The US rewarded him with the opportunity to live a quiet life in New York. But it did not include access to a job. He struggled for years to find an employer who would trust him with more than menial work. NSSI was his salvation.

When Yazeen saw how the Commander had realigned Mirror 170 to help the Maldives tourist resorts, he reported it to Chris and Jordan. They immediately recognized moneymaking possibilities.

Jordan redirected NSSI's staff to take advantage of this new opportunity. They studied the SSP Master

Plan maps to see what other tourist sites might be shadowed in the northern winter season.

They contacted the largest tropical tourist resorts in the shadowed areas and explained the shadow's potential impact from an SSP mirror orbiting overhead. They offered the resort a solution for a substantial fee, assuring the operator that NSSI had unique access to the SSPC to realign the mirror immediately. NSSI did not explain the origin of this capability or what other tourist locations were affected.

Savvy customers understood this arrangement would not involve any public review of the realignment. They didn't want to know if the realignments were legal, or if bribery was involved.

Fixing things for one area inevitably moved the shadow somewhere else nearby. So if area A was unwilling to pay, area B might. The risk to A if it didn't pay was that NSSI would take steps to benefit area B, regardless of the consequences for area A. This externality was inherent in the SSP design.

Some customers signed up to get out from under a shadow. NSSI realigned the relevant mirror to improve the sunlight hours in their locations. They used their clone of CDI's Emergency Terminal to give MSTY instructions that were verbatim copies of Commander Fauré's instructions for Mirror 170.

Other customers paid to avoid the risk of being shadowed if a competitor paid NSSI for a realignment. In that case, NSSI didn't need to move anything. It merely promised not to sign contracts with others that would be injurious. NSSI was getting paid *not* to realign a mirror for someone else. It was a classic insurance protection racket.

Jordan and Chris knew, of course, that criminal laws everywhere treat obtaining money or property from a party by threatening to damage that party as "extortion" or blackmail.

The law of New York, where NSSI was incorporated, would apply. Moreover, the US Federal "Racketeer Influenced and Corrupt Organizations Act," known as RICO, makes anyone involved in an organization that commits extortion under the applicable State law also guilty of a Federal crime.

∞∞∞

When Yazeen saw that MSTY had added a videocall with CDI to Commander Fauré's calendar for 5 February 2035, he promptly reported it to Jordan and Chris.

Chris had already been worried about the risks posed by CDI. "If CDI ever discovers that NSSI misrepresented our relationship with SSPC, they will send the police after us in a hurry. Because unless CDI can persuade the authorities that NSSI misrepresented their authority to hack MSTY, CDI itself will likely be prosecuted and convicted for illegally hacking MSTY."

Chris's fears multiplied after Yazeen's news. He warned Jordan, "If CDI discovers that we've moved Mirrors 210, 220, and 226 and tells Fauré, our access will end instantly. The Commander will quickly learn who we are from CDI. We'll be arrested for extortion and hacking a UN computer system."

Jordan didn't think that possibility was very plausible. "If CDI concludes we misled them, they will simply shut down their SSP operation and insist it never happened. Why get entangled in a complex legal and factual dispute with NSSI and the UN?

"If the authorities ask us, we will dispute every statement they make about our claim to represent SSPC IT. CDI never asked to see our alleged contract with SSPC. They certainly can't produce a copy. If the prosecution doesn't believe CDI's innocence, they could be sentenced to years in prison, even if we are too."

Jordan succeeded in calming Chris down. But after giving the matter more thought, Jordan saw a different reason to change their approach.

"Chris, I agree we are in danger. And we've probably exhausted the prospects for making more money with this trick. We've already made a lot of money and can afford to disappear. Maybe it's time to get out without leaving a trace.

"How does going back to Moscow sound? It's a heterogeneous population, and people's suspicious, self-protective attitude makes it a convenient place to disappear."

Chris quickly warmed to the idea. "I agree; it's time to retire and live on our winnings. I've been thinking we might make some quick money a different way. We can send the Commander an anonymous message demanding that he wire funds to our South Sudan bank. Otherwise, we'll expose his repositioning of Mirror 170.

He'll probably think it's coming from CDI, but he'll comply to avoid exposure. If it works, we'll divide up the money.

Jordan liked the idea. "We can do it from Moscow. If it doesn't work, we'll be no worse off. CDI will be the most likely suspect. They'll be caught entirely off guard. I doubt they know we've hacked them or the Emergency Terminal or moved any mirrors. So they'll be scrambling to defend themselves against charges of responsibility for the mirrors and the blackmail. Their whole business will collapse if word gets out that they are even suspected of hacking the SSPC.

"I've had another thought. The right people in Moscow might be interested in learning how to hack MSTY. It could be useful for threatening any tropical country, and Russia has no love for this UN project anyway."

Chris promptly assembled the staff to inform them of the end of NSSI. He laid out the plans for winding up NSSI.

"It's time to shut down everything, physically and financially. NSSI and its staff must entirely disappear. Where you go is your own decision. I strongly recommend you leave the United States, or at least New York State, as soon as possible.

"NSSI has enough funds to give each of you a farewell bonus of a year's salary for your relocation. You are welcome to take your computer, phone, and other personal items."

The staff was surprised and disturbed, but they appreciated the generous severance terms. They immediately began dismantling the office and making plans for new lives elsewhere.

Chris was still not feeling secure. "At this point," he told Jordan, "no one knows anything about NSSI, but that will quickly change. We've left too much information out in the open in our tourism contacts. Once CDI begins cooperating, the official investigators will easily trace our paths.

"I think our long-run security depends on terminating the CDI operation before they even know what we are doing."

Jordan was surprised. "Isn't that pretty extreme?"

Chris responded sharply, "CDI is a danger to us as long as it has its computer systems and files. We need to get rid of them. I suggest we send Yazeen to destroy their computers and files as soon as possible."

"How would you have him do it?"

"However—he's the expert on destruction. Leave that to him. The less we know, the better."

"I see your point. Okay, but no physical harm to anyone."

"Agreed. I'll get him started immediately."

Chris met with Yazeen. "I know you are more worried about your future than most of the staff. We have a unique assignment for you. We will pay you handsomely to make CDI's records and computers disappear.

"I've been to their headquarters in Wuhan, and I can lay out the physical location. How you terminate their operations is up to you. You know more about such matters than I do. There will be money upfront and a bonus once you finish. We don't want any personal injury; just destroy their files and computer systems."

Yazeen was reluctant to re-engage his former skills as an ISIS soldier. He wanted no part of destruction ever again. But without this NSSI job, he didn't have any employment options. He was a mediocre computer tech, and finding a satisfactory new job would be complicated, especially now, without favorable references.

The next day he met again with Chris. "I'll do it, with the understanding that I'm not expected to hurt anyone. I can end their operational capability.

"I insist on at least ₣200,000 in advance and ample funds—at least ₣ 100,000—for hardware, travel, and other expenses. If that's not agreeable, you'll need to find someone else."

Chris smiled. "No problem. We don't want any bloodshed either. We just want their computers and files rendered useless."

"When do I leave?"

"As soon as possible. The ₣300,000 will be in your account in an hour."

Chapter 14

Cai vs. Fauré

AS 1900 ON 5 FEBRUARY 2035 approached, Cai sat anxiously at her computer. *I wonder if the Commander has even noticed this call on his schedule. How will he react to an unexpected image on his Emergency Terminal? I guess I'll know in a few seconds.*

She opened the keyhole to the Commander's Emergency Terminal and began the call. In a moment, she heard what she assumed was the Commander's voice. She knew he could see her, but he didn't activate his video image.

Commander Fauré was startled when the Emergency Terminal came to life. It had never opened by itself before. His reaction was about as Cai predicted. He instantly began shouting, "Who the hell are you? And how did you gain access to this terminal? I can have this videocall traced, you know, and you should also know that breaking into the SSPC computer system is a crime."

Cai spoke softly and calmly. "Good afternoon, Commander. My name is Cai Jin, and I am a co-founder of Computer Defense, Incorporated of Wuhan, China, also known as CDI. All our personnel are former officers in the cybersecurity unit of the Chinese Aerospace Command.

"Network Security Systems Incorporated, known as NSSI, a New York cybersecurity firm, hired us as a subcontractor on a contract with your Command. They asked us to help search for a keyhole in the SSPC computer system that hackers might exploit.

"As you can see, we did find a keyhole through your Emergency Terminal, which gave us access to MSTY and your restricted files."

Commander Fauré was every bit as shocked, angry, and confounded as Cai had hoped.

"Hold on right there!" he spluttered. "I don't have any idea who you are or who this NSSI outfit is. To the best of my knowledge, we have not contracted out any cybersecurity work. Is this some kind of shakedown?"

"Absolutely not, sir. We were worried about the possibility that NSSI was not connected with SSPC when they hired us. We insisted on speaking to an SSPC representative to vouch for them.

"NSSI brought Christopher Kangata to our office to vouch for NSSI. His credentials identified him as an employee of SSPC IT. He is the SSPC manager of the cybersecurity contract with NSSI.

"Have you heard of Chris? He's from Kenya, and he is certainly knowledgeable about SSPC and your cybersecurity program."

"I repeat. I have not heard about any cybersecurity contracting effort, and I would have to know about it.

Our IT Director reports directly to me, and he is not authorized to sign contracts without my permission."

Neither Cai nor the Commander said anything for an instant, each trying to absorb unexpected information about NSSI. Now Cai was the curious one. Afraid the Commander might end the call, Cai quickly began speaking to fill the void.

"Then I'm even happier I called you in this unorthodox way. If you are willing to confirm that NSSI is not one of your contractors and let me know, we will not deliver any of our work to them. Whatever they are up to, they won't get any help from us.

"I also wanted to talk to you in person about some information we found in the files on your use of your Emergency Terminal. You directed MSTY to alter the perpendicular deviation of Mirror 170 incrementally in 20 monthly steps without anyone knowing about it.

"According to your calendar, you took that action shortly after you met with Director Ibrahim, from the Maldives, which is partly located under Mirror 170 and would be shadowed during the winter months. Your alteration of the mirror's perpendicular deviation would seem to be an effort to remedy that shadowing.

"The SSPC Manual prescribes the procedures for altering the SSP Master Plan, but you circumvented them and moved Mirror 170 immediately, without notice to the public or even the relevant SSPC personnel.

"It certainly looks like a favor to one Director, and it's hard not to surmise there might have been a reciprocal favor in exchange, perhaps for your personal benefit. If that were the case, we believe our duty as citizens would require us to report this matter to the UN accounting and ethics officers.

"As I mentioned, our firm's owners are all former Chinese Air Force computer officers. We felt that the sensitivity of our finding required us to discuss it directly with you before sharing anything with NSSI or anyone else.

"Perhaps you can explain what this Mirror 170 activity was all about."

Commander Fauré grimaced.

Should I tell her the whole story? Isn't that admitting damaging facts? But she has obtained the files, so I can't deny the facts.

Speaking slowly, in a matter-of-fact manner, he recited his defense.

"I can see how my action could create an appearance of impropriety, but nothing could be further from the truth. Director Ibrahim came to see me with an urgent concern. Although the mirrors had only been in place a short time, he reported that tourist bookings in the Maldives were already suffering.

"Resorts in other locations were spreading rumors that the Maldives resorts would be in the shadows of an SSP mirror all winter. Shadows might fall on some other resorts as well. The World Bank financed some of these enterprises, and thousands of jobs depend on them, directly and indirectly.

"The SSPC technical models indicated that the mirror shadows would have only the most minimal effect on weather conditions for agriculture, fishing, and other primary economic activities. But the difference between the prediction of a cloudless gray day and a bright sunny day is critical for tourist resorts from a marketing standpoint.

"I assured Ibrahim I would look into the matter and take what action I could to ensure the effect would be minimal at worst. The shadow maps did show the Maldives resort areas would be shadowed in the coming winter months, as he feared.

"As you know, I asked MSTY what realignment would be necessary to undo that effect and whether it would affect the achievement of SSP's goals. MSTY concluded the impact of the required changes in Mirror 170's perpendicular deviation would be so minimal that it would be lost in the rounding of the measurement numbers. In other words, it would have no discernable effect whatsoever on the global climate.

"My job as Commander is to ensure that the SSPC and SSP avoid damage to any UN Member's wellbeing, which includes making minute changes that are unlikely to have any effect whatsoever on agriculture, fisheries, or other significant human activities.

"Overlooking the hypothetical shadow effects on tourist facilities was a technical error, and it was vital to begin correcting it without delay. The procedures for making a formal change in the SSP would take much too long to save the tourist resorts from financial collapse.

"I can assure you that no financial benefit came to me or anyone, so far as I know. I don't know any way to demonstrate that negative fact to you. You'll just need to take my word for it."

Cai thought for a moment before responding. "Nevertheless, you ignored the specific protocols for changing the Master Plan. Assuming you acted in good faith, the protocols still must be respected.

"Can you promise me that you will direct MSTY to undo the changes you ordered? In that case, CDI will have nothing to report."

The Commander struggled to find an answer.

I've got to offer to do something. But what? At least I can get some time.

Faure responded equivocally. "I'm not sure you have anything to report. I am convinced that the changes I made were the kind of very minor, routine adjustments that the SSPC Manual gives me the discretion to make. It might have been wiser to follow the protocol for adjusting the Master Plan even though it is not legally required, but it's too late for that now.

"The delicate character of the mirrors means that every movement creates stresses on their surfaces and the connections with their central structures. We can only move them slowly and incrementally. That's why MSTY and I concluded that the adjustments should be made over many months.

"I'll consult with MSTY about how long it would take to move Mirror 170 back to its original position without damage. We can't afford to lose a mirror. Once I have the facts, I'll decide whether it makes any sense to undo the changes. The shortest time for a moving Mirror 170 safely is likely to be most of two years.

"In the meantime, I'll continue to explore whether to begin public review of the Master Plan. The review would address how to accomplish the desired result for tourist facilities in locations that seem likely to suffer possible adverse consequences from mirror shadows. It will include further studies to identify other shadow effects that might justify adjustments.

"It would be a mistake to announce that the SSPC is considering changes to the Master Plan before we know which changes might be necessary and whether making them would be consistent with our mission. I'm sure I can satisfy your concerns without injuring the Maldives resorts or the functions or reputation of the SSPC."

Cai smiled inside, but she maintained a stern countenance for the Commander's screen.

"When can I expect to talk with you again?"

"I think two weeks should give me time to pull together some of the information you want. Then we can talk about what is possible in adjusting the SSP Master Plan as necessary."

Cai thought for a minute about the Commander's response.

"I guess that's probably the best you can do. I'll call you again at 1900 your time on Friday, 20 February, on this Emergency Terminal. I hope you will be willing to show your face next time. We're trying to be your friends."

Fauré thought about asking Cai to turn off CDI's Emergency Terminal clone and stop illegally monitoring MSTY.

But at this point, I have no other channel of communication with her. And maybe it will be to my advantage to have their illegal activity continue.

Fauré said nothing more, and Cai ended the call.

ꝏꝏꝏ

Cai was pleased to have learned so much in the conversation with Fauré. She reported every detail to Zhang, again in her office with the computer off. Zhang found the Commander's assertion that NSSI had no contract with SSPC astounding.

"You mean this whole exercise, including the monthly payments, is part of a fraud? NSSI wanted us to find a keyhole so they could exploit it for their own profit? That's outrageous! And we were dupes, aiding their criminal scheme.

"We must notify them immediately that we are ending our relationship. We will not give them the results of our work, and we will not refund their money.

"If they make a fuss, we'll turn them over to the Ministry of State Security. I suppose we should also report them to the UN IT Security department."

Cai, who already had more opportunity to think about what to do next, counseled caution.

"Not necessarily. For all we know at this point, the Commander was lying to me to save himself.

"He may be canceling his contract with NSSI right now, telling them to disappear. I'm expecting that the next time I talk to Fauré, he will have his IT and security people tracing the call and investigating us and NSSI.

"I didn't explicitly promise not to do anything public for the next two weeks, though that was undoubtedly our understanding. We need to investigate further even before we get more answers from the Commander. Maybe we can verify or disprove his story.

"And I want him to tell us what he is willing to do to remedy his questionable conduct."

∞∞∞

Neither Cai nor Fauré imagined that NSSI was eavesdropping on their conversation via NSSI's Emergency Terminal clone. When Cai ended the call, Jordan and Chris looked at each other and nodded their heads wordlessly.

"Well, Chris, we've made the right decision to close down and leave without a trace. They will be looking for us. I hope Yazeen is successful, and you should urge him to speed up. But we can't wait for his return before we disappear."

Chris raised a different question. "Do you think we should forget the idea of demanding ₣15,000,000 from the Commander? Every communication with SSPC gives them another chance to trace us."

"Let's see if we can get him to wire us the money, or at least some of it. We'll be in Moscow by then, and they're unlikely to find us there.

"Agreed."

Chapter 15

Extortion!

FAURÉ'S IMMEDIATE IMPULSE after the surprise conversation with Cai was to talk to Jerry Stephens, his IT Director, about the CDI and NSSI. But he quickly recognized he needed to know everything that had transpired on the Emergency Terminal before he did anything.

Then I'll need to confirm everything I've heard from Cai about NSSI and CDI. And I need how to handle Ibrahim if I decide to start reversing the changes to Mirror 170. I need to develop a plan to dig out of this mess.

After a day spent evaluating possible paths forward, Commander Fauré began to implement his strategy. He opened the Emergency Terminal and gave MSTY two simple directions: "First, please tell me all uses of the Emergency Terminal and by whom. Second, prepare a summary of all documents in my confidential files and a list of who got access to them and when they did.

MSTY responded to the first request instantly.

"You have used the Emergency Terminal eight times. The first was on 1 May 2033. The second use was three days later, when you instructed me to adjust the perpendicular deviation of Mirror 170.

"Six others have occurred in the last two months. One asked me to put the 5 February videocall with Cai Jin on your calendar.

"The others asked me to adjust the perpendicular deviation of Mirrors 210, 220, and 226. My records show that you made all of them. You also asked me to prepare a summary of the documents in your confidential files. The documents all came from you, according to my records."

Fauré was horrified. Someone had hacked MSTY and was moving other mirrors, and he didn't even know about it. Everything seemed out of control.

After regaining his composure, he gave MSTY more instructions. "MSTY, I have not sent you any messages through this Emergency Terminal except those in 2033. The others were made by someone else, making unauthorized use of my password and previous instructions.

"First, please change my password to something else right now and send the new one to me. And only put it in my confidential file." MSTY instantly changed his password and sent him the new one.

"Second, please study the messages you received in the last three months to see if you can distinguish their origin. They were all unauthorized. Did they all come from the same computer? It would be helpful if you could find a way to trace those inputs back to the sources."

"Third, don't make any more realignment adjustments to any mirrors. Please leave them exactly where they are right now. Thank you."

Fauré's head was spinning.

Why would some young computer jocks in China want to start moving mirrors around? Cai Jin said NSSI only hired them to find a keyhole, not move mirrors. Was she lying? Did CDI also move Mirrors 210, 220, and 226? Or does someone else have access to MSTY now?

I need to look at the maps and see what locations are affected and how. Maybe I can ask Ibrahim if he knows anything about these other areas. Or maybe not.

He asked MSTY for maps of these mirrors' shadows. They were near other major tourist destinations.

- Mirror 210: Hainan Island, off China
- Mirror 220: Halong Bay, Vietnam
- Mirror 226: Phuket, Thailand

But none of them were directly under a shadow, so why would they be so concerned? As he ate his usual spartan dinner in the SSPC Officers Mess, he struggled to understand the point of moving the other mirrors. He thought about asking MSTY for her hypothesis in the morning.

Finally, he realized the crucial flaw in his map review. MSTY had given him maps of the *current* shadows of Mirrors 170, 210, 220, and 226. Those shadows were near but not over the tourist destinations.

The maps weren't showing the *original* shadows. Fauré should be examining the shadows as the Master Plan had initially aligned the mirrors.

He asked MSTY for the necessary information to test his theory.

"MSTY, please give me maps that show the shadows when the original zero perpendicular deviations for these mirrors were still in effect. Are they over tourist resorts?

MSTY took two days to complete her much more detailed, evidence-based analysis. Her answer was an unequivocal yes, with maps and data supporting her conclusions. Commander Fauré now understood the rationale of whoever moved the shadows to benefit the affected locations. Presumably, they got paid by someone.

It looks like CDI is playing a two-faced game. Once they learned what I had done for the Maldives, it would be easy to see the business opportunity. Contact the other tourist sites, explain the threat from the shadows, and offer to make them go away.

Then accuse me of misconduct benefitting Director Ibrahim and Maldives. They expected that threat would lead me to hide their realignments of Mirrors 210, 220, and 226.

I won't let them get away with these crimes, even at the risk of my career.

∞∞∞

As the Commander was mulling over exactly how to respond to this threat, the Emergency Terminal opened. Several days had passed since his conversation with Cai, but he was not expecting another call from her until 20 February.

But this time, the Terminal did not display Cai Jin or anyone—simply a message:

> WE HAVE COPIED THE MATERIALS IN YOUR CLASSIFIED FILES. WE ARE WILLING TO DESTROY THESE COMPROMISING DOCUMENTS, KEEP NO COPIES, AND INFORM NO ONE.
> SEND A PAYMENT OF ₣15,000,000 BY WIRE TRANSFER TO ACCOUNT NUMBER 10100 5621 7628 AT BANK SWIFT NUMBER 0154 88453 WITHIN 14 DAYS.

Commander Fauré could not believe what he was reading. The movement of Mirrors 210, 220, and 226 had already radically changed his plan for the upcoming conversation with Cai. This blackmail would change it even more.

Ms. Cai, who seemed so honorable and reasonable, turns out to be a blackmailer! My silence isn't enough. She wants cash! Even if I had the money, I'm not paying anyone hush money to hide a decision I still think was reasonable.

If I pay with SSPC funds, the Governing Board Members will soon find the transaction and suspend me pending a full inquiry. And then they would probably fire me for misconduct.

I need UN Security Management Services (SMS) to help me respond to this extortion. SMS might even be willing to pay some of the money as a device to track down the blackmailers.

Once SMS sees the files, they will also want to investigate my treatment of the Maldives. I believe responding to the Director's urgent request was appropriate, but I can see how a review board could reach a different conclusion. I did circumvent the standard procedures for amending the Master Plan. And I hid my action, which arguably shows I knew it was wrong.

SMS is likely to investigate on its own before it does anything. I can't afford to wait. I need to do more to resolve this matter myself. I will respond forcefully to CDI's outrageous demands and stop any further tampering with our mirrors.

This tangle could end my aspirations and even my military career. But I'm only 52, with a life ahead of me. I won't give up without a fight.

Commander Fauré called SMS Director Wang Shu. The UN Master Computer took his name and asked about the subject of the call. "That is confidential. SSPC needs immediate assistance to deal with a cybersecurity breach. I will explain the matter in full to Director Wang."

Matching the Commander's name with a list of high-ranking UN officials, the Master Computer replied, "Please hold. Let me see if the Director can take your call."

In about five minutes, Director Wang came on. "It's a pleasure to talk to you, Commander. How can I help you?"

Fauré outlined the Emergency Terminal hack; the unauthorized repositioning of Mirrors 210, 220, and 226; and the blackmail demand. He briefly mentioned that he had himself moved Mirror 170 to alleviate an urgent economic hardship.

He knew Wang was deeply sympathetic to the SSP mission. In 2025, when the UN Security Council debated Russia's claimed invasion of its airspace and natural resource rights by the tropospheric veil experiment, Wang led Singapore's defense of the project. She instantly became a celebrity for her persuasive defense of global action on climate disruption. She was a role model for young women everywhere seeking and pursuing diplomatic careers.

Fauré explained the current and ultimate risks created by this hack.

"So far, these hackers have just been lining their pockets by extorting tourist resort owners. But they'll soon realize that ruthless governments could use or threaten to use this power against rivals or uncooperative neighbors. And they will pay handsomely for the access key.

"If this abuse ever becomes public, the result would be widespread demands to scrap the whole solar shield initiative. Those who initially opposed the effort, from unhappy governments to environmental and scientific purists, would claim vindication. We have no idea what would happen to the climate if the shield suddenly disappeared."

Wang instantly understood the seriousness of the problem. She offered the assistance of her best investigator. "You need someone who speaks Chinese as well as English. Fortunately, Inspector Cheng Yiming, perhaps our most talented investigator, meets that requirement. Quiet, patient, thorough, trustworthy.

"I urge you to take him completely into your confidence and tell him everything. I'll make sure he understands what is at stake. This investigation is not about investigating or protecting you; it's about protecting SSPC, the SSP, and the reputation of the whole UN organization."

"Thank you. I will certainly cooperate fully with Cheng and work to get this matter resolved promptly and quietly."

I wonder just how Inspector Cheng will react to his adjustment of Mirror 170. Regardless, I must tell him the whole story. He's a skilled professional investigator. He will inevitably see all my Emergency Terminal files.

Stonewalling or hiding anything from him is likely to fail, and the consequences for my career and the SSPC could be fatal.

Nevertheless, Fauré felt a deep sense of relief, now that he had allies and could see a path out of the thicket he had created.

Chapter 16

Fauré Fights Exposure

FAURÉ THEN BEGAN EXECUTING his plan for avoiding a personal and organizational calamity. He called in Jerry Stephens.

"Jerry, I have received information that we have contracted with a firm called NSSI—Network Security Systems Incorporated or something like that—to help us ensure that no one can hack MSTY. I don't recall approving any outside contracts. Am I mistaken?"

"No, sir. We've talked to some outside contractors about helping us look for keyholes, but we haven't decided to recommend that yet. I wouldn't think of selecting or contracting with anyone without consulting you. I'm not authorized to sign any contract without your sign-off. Why do you ask?"

"A Chinese company called Computer Defense Inc.—CDI—told me that we have a contract with NSSI and NSSI had subcontracted some work to them. Have you ever heard of either of them?"

"Never, sir. We're actively evaluating possible contractors for this work with Procurement, and I'm thoroughly familiar with everyone in the field. I would've heard of NSSI. I wouldn't know CDI because we wouldn't retain a Chinese company for security reasons, but I've never heard their name either."

"Okay. Please see what you can learn about both companies and report back by the end of the week. And please see if anyone at the UN knows a computer specialist named Christopher Kangata or something like it, from Kenya, who allegedly claimed to work for us."

"Yes, sir. I'll get on it immediately. It shouldn't be hard to find out about any reputable company in the field. They are all hunting for business from UN organizations. And I'm sure I've never met any Kenyan in this field, in or out of the UN agencies."

"Thank you."

Two days later, Stephens reported back. "No one has ever heard of NSSI, Network Security Systems Incorporated, or Christopher Kangata. I have found some information on CDI. It's a new but well-respected Chinese firm, set up by young alumni of the Chinese Air & Space Command's Computer Center in Wuhan.

"This folder has more detail on CDI, its location, and bios of the founders. We haven't had any dealings with them, directly or indirectly."

"Thank you. That's helpful. If you learn anything more, please let me know promptly."

∞∞∞

In their morning meeting two days later, the Commander asked Jay about Kelly's investigation into the repositioning of Mirror 170.

"I'm glad you asked, sir. Officer O'Rourke did contact me because she was disappointed not to have heard from you or me about her Memorandum. She is scrupulously following your direction not to talk to anyone about her findings. She only shared this data with me because she hoped to arrange another conversation with you.

"She was curious about whether the repositioning of Mirror 170 was unique. She reviewed all the data in MSTY's files and found similar marginal realignments of three other mirrors—numbers 210, 220, and 226. Again, no alerts or warnings from MSTY.

"Would you like to talk with her?"

Fauré feigned surprise.

"So three other mirrors have been repositioned? That's certainly interesting. Yes, I suppose I should talk with her. Can she come by later today?"

"I imagine so, sir. I can't think of anything she would consider a higher priority. I'll invite her up as soon as we are finished."

"Good. By the way, I've learned more about Officer O'Rourke's history through informal channels. She's not quite the straight arrow the official records suggest. I hope you won't put yourself in a vulnerable position with her. I need your independent, objective judgment."

"Yes, sir. I'm fully aware of the need to avoid being compromised."

Fifteen minutes later, Kelly received a videocall from Jay. Her adrenalin began flowing.

He's never called again since . . .

Jay was brief and all business. "Hello. The Commander asked about you this morning. I told him about the results of your new research. He seemed interested. He'd like to meet with you in his office this afternoon. How soon can you come up?"

"Right now, I guess. Did he say why he wants to talk to me?"

"No. I've told you everything I know."

"I guess I'll find out soon enough. I'll be there in 30 minutes."

Kelly rushed to the restroom to freshen her makeup and straighten up her uniform. Her mind said she wanted to look her best for the Commander, but her heart was hoping she might see Jay again.

She rode the elevator to the top floor and paced slowly down the hallway to the Commander's office. Jay was nowhere to be seen. She announced her presence to MSTY and turned to sit down. After a moment during which MSTY alerted the Commander, MSTY directed her to enter his office.

Commander Fauré was waiting for her impatiently. He seemed wary and uncomfortable. Kelly suddenly felt that it had been a mistake to make herself look attractive—it wasn't the image she needed right now.

Kelly saw the Commander's whole office for the first time. The walls were an appropriate space blue. One held diplomas, citations, and photos of Commander Fauré. Two others displayed large images of Space Shield Mirror launches and drawings of their subsequent assembly and deployment in orbit. The view of the East River and Brooklyn through his office windows was even more mesmerizing.

Fauré had disabled the full-time video recording system in his office without mentioning it to Kelly. He wanted this conversation entirely off the record.

"Good morning. First, my congratulations on passing your exams. Your scores were among the best anyone has ever achieved. So welcome to the SSPC as an Officer.

"Jay just told me you found that three other mirrors were also adjusted slightly. What inspired you to investigate other mirrors? Did anyone suggest this to you?"

Kelly's brief surge of pride at the Commander's recognition of her outstanding test results quickly melted. She detected his displeasure from his demeanor and tone.

"No, sir. My research was entirely my idea. I wondered if any other mirrors had been moved and if MSTY treated them the same way. The answer to both questions was yes. When I asked MSTY who authorized the moves, she declined to answer on confidentiality grounds. I thought the Manual rules are clear that only you could authorize such an action, and only with full transparency."

"Who have you talked to about these changes? Anyone at all?"

"Just Jay. I told him to explain why I wanted another conversation with you, or at least he should let you know what I had found. I thought it was important, but that may be a mistake."

"You realize, Officer O'Rourke, that I directed you not to talk to anyone else about your findings. I didn't make an exception for talking to Jay. I expect you to take my orders literally.

"I looked into your background after our last meeting. The Irish Air Force Personnel Office whitewashed your record to facilitate your reassignment here. Your past behavior includes excessive drug and alcohol use, casual sex with foreigners, and other potential security weaknesses and vulnerabilities.

"Moreover, there is reason to suspect that, in violation of the flight training program rules, you became pregnant while you were in flight school. That's why you couldn't cope with the pilot training test those days and why you thought you could pass it later. But you couldn't say so explicitly in your formal appeal because it also showed a violation of the rules."

Kelly was staggered by the Commander's knowledge of her past. She was far more exposed than she had imagined. Now she was afraid for both herself and Jay.

OMG, he knows I was pregnant! Where did he get this information? I need to stick to the truth; any lie would be the end.

"So here you are," Fauré continued. "This assignment is your last chance for a military career. I could dismiss you from SSPC right this moment as a security risk.

"However, your test scores and your inquisitiveness and persistence display valuable qualities. You're older now, and I'm willing to assume you won't repeat past mistakes. So I'm willing to consider gambling on you and allowing you to redeem yourself."

Kelly felt relieved for an instant, until she realized the Commander was still not finished.

"So now I'm going to ask my questions again. Please correct anything you said that wasn't accurate and complete. Did anyone ask or inspire you to do this analysis? Does anyone know about it besides Jay and me? Does MSTY know your conclusions? Could anyone else have learned about your conclusions without your knowing it?"

"Sir, I stand by my answers about the mirrors. It was my curiosity that inspired the research, no one else. So far as I know, aside from you, Jay, and MSTY, no one knows that I did any research or what I learned. That is the whole story.

"As for my past conduct, I have been completely loyal to the SSPC. I've done nothing that could be damaging to you or the organization. I certainly didn't and don't intend to do any harm."

The Commander sat back in his chair.

That's what she says. She could be part of some scheme to destroy this whole enterprise or even an unwitting agent of a hostile group or government. But I have no evidence of that. Dismissing her would just create an enemy. Anyway, she's bright and inquisitive and already knows too much. She's a potential risk, but at this point, I think it's better to trust her.

He continued in a more conversational tone.

"All right. I'm going to trust you, and I expect your full support and loyalty. You told me about Mirror 170, but I didn't know anything about the other mirrors.

Someone hacked MSTY through my Emergency Terminal. It doesn't have the same security as the other terminals because the designers assumed I would be the only one with physical access. That seems to have been an error.

"MSTY assumed any message she received through the Emergency Terminal came from me, and she followed it. The hackers probably moved those mirrors as part of a criminal scheme. However they are profiting from it, we must stop it. I may need your help to solve this mystery.

"You and Jay are the only SSPC personnel I am trusting on this matter. I am relying on your absolute loyalty to the SSPC mission. And please keep your relationship with Jay completely professional, because you will be working together on this matter."

Kelly didn't know what to think. *Does he already know about my night with Jay, too? I don't dare ask any questions. One wrong word could make things worse.*

"Thank you, sir. I appreciate your trust and confidence in me. I will do my loyal best for you and the SSPC in any way you direct."

"I'm betting on that," the Commander replied as he rose to usher her out.

Chapter 17

Fauré vs. Cai

RIGHT ON SCHEDULE, AT 1900 on 20 February, Cai appeared again on the Fauré's Emergency Terminal.

"Good evening, Commander! I see your video is still blocked. I was hoping to see your face, so our discussions could proceed more openly. As you can tell, we got your new password. I'm eager to hear what steps you have taken to remedy your secret action to realign Mirror 170."

"I'm here, and I've initiated the amendment procedure," Fauré replied angrily.

"But I'm not going to play games with you. You claimed to be working for SSPC as a subcontractor of ours, exploring possible weaknesses in our computer security system. You said an SSPC IT Department employee named Christopher Kangata vouched for NSSI.

"Jerry Stephens, my IT Director, assured me we have no cybersecurity contractors. He cannot find any record of Network Security Systems Incorporated or NSSI beyond the plain vanilla articles of incorporation.

He also determined that no one named Christopher Kangata or any Chris or anyone from Kenya exists in SSPC or anywhere in any UN IT offices.

"At this point, I must assume you made up all that. Since your last call, I reviewed my personal files on MSTY to see what messages have come through the Emergency Terminal. I see you've been busy. You sent MSTY orders in my name to realign Mirrors 210, 220, and 226. I can only assume that you profited from those actions.

"Then you got even more greedy. Three days ago, you sent a demand that I deposit ₣ 15,000,000 in a numbered bank account in 14 days. Otherwise, you would release my confidential documents to the media.

"Are you so naïve as to think that blunt extortion would work? Where do you think I would get that kind of money?"

As Fauré talked, Inspector Cheng was sitting next to him, listening in on the call. Simultaneously, Cheng's computer support expert, Natan Carmell, was tracing the incoming videocall's source.

Cai was flabbergasted by the Commander's attack. She paused to suppress her shock and collect her thoughts.

My reply must be calm, articulate, and persuasive, or he will never speak to me again, and CDI will be in deep trouble.

"Commander, I have no idea what you are talking about! All I know is that you moved Mirror 170. I don't know anything about realigning Mirrors 210, 220, or 226, or any blackmail demand.

"My partners and I spent years in the People's Air Force. We are honorable, ethical citizens. We would never think of doing anything like what you describe. Moreover, it would kill our thriving business if we got caught or were even suspected.

"As I said in my first call, we found your activities while we were looking for cybersecurity vulnerabilities in the SSPC system. We did this work under an agreement with NSSI, which we thought was your contractor.

"We found a keyhole in the loose restrictions on the use of your Emergency Terminal. We were about to report the keyhole to NSSI when we realized that NSSI could conceivably misuse that information. We decided to talk to you first. I videocalled you to get your explanation for repositioning Mirror 170.

"Are you telling me that NSSI isn't your contractor? Before we agreed to take this assignment, we insisted that someone from SSPC IT vouch for NSSI in person. Christopher Kangata visited us, along with Jordan Milhaus of NSSI.

"Mr. Kangata presented his SSPC IT credentials, explained why SSPC wanted the work NSSI was asking us to do, why it was important to SSPC, and why the utmost secrecy was necessary. NSSI has paid us monthly, in substantial amounts, on schedule, for several months."

Then Cai fell silent. Fauré pondered Cai's response. He decided to test her legitimacy by demanding her cooperation.

"If what you are saying is true, we are both victims of NSSI's fraud. We need to work together to get to the truth. Let me send my Executive Assistant, Officer Sanjay Bhattachar, and one or two others to Wuhan to talk with you and inspect the relevant documents.

Jay reads and speaks Chinese fluently. He will want to talk with you and your staff in detail about what he found in my Emergency Terminal files. I assume you are still in Wuhan. How can he reach you there?"

"Yes, we are in Wuhan. He can call me when he arrives. I'm sending you my videocall URL right now. Your people should stay at the "Nice to Meet You Apartment Hotel" on Bayi Road in the Wuchang District. It's walking distance from our office, which is in the Dong Hu building on Huanshan South Road. I'll tell the hotel you are coming.

"Zhang Xingwen, the other founding partner, and I will be available to talk and work with your people to discover the facts. I will immediately collect all the payment and contract documents from NSSI for their inspection. I hope to be able to document everything for your Assistant when he arrives."

While Cai was talking, Natan informed Cheng he succeeded in tracing Cai's computer. Cheng signaled Fauré that the call could end any time.

Cai continued, "What you have described makes me think that someone has hacked our internal network. I can't think of any other way anyone else is likely to have accessed your Emergency Terminal as we did. It took us several months to find the keyhole. I'm confident no one at CDI did anything wrong."

Commander Fauré responded, "Thank you. I appreciate your cooperation. We need to work together on this puzzle to protect both of our reputations. We'll talk further after Jay returns from Wuhan."

ooooo

Fauré ended the call and turned to Cheng. "Did we get everything we needed?"

"Well, Natan got what he needed. And we heard what Cai has to say. If she's lying, she's pretty good at it. It's certainly possible that this 'Christopher Kangata' and NSSI misled her and her colleagues.

"Natan is checking to see if he can trace the computers that ordered realignment of the mirrors. That would tell us whether they came from Cai's computer."

"If he can identify other computers, I'll be surprised. MSTY didn't even detect any sign that Cai's terminal or the blackmailers' terminal were different from mine.

"I see your point, Commander. It does suggest that Cai is not lying, and someone hacked her system. NSSI, whoever they are, would have every reason to hack CDI to protect their investment. I think you need to tell MSTY to confirm with you orally every time she receives any instructions through the Emergency Terminal."

Fauré agreed. "Unfortunately, we can't shut down the Emergency Terminal right now. We need to maintain a communications link with the blackmailers to videocall the Emergency Terminal to discuss money and extend their deadline. It's not in their interest to release the documents so long as they think they still might get their money."

Cheng looked at his phone and turned to Fauré.

"Apparently Natan knows tricks that MSTY hasn't been taught yet. He was able to differentiate the terminals by looking at the relay links. Cai's computer is located in China, as we expected. But other messages came from New York City, and the blackmail message came from a computer in Moscow."

Fauré turned pale at the thought that Russia or any other government might already have access to the mirrors.

If Russia acquires this capability, the whole Space Shield is at risk. They could destroy the effectiveness of the entire system or move selected mirrors for their own advantage. Merely knowing about the security breach would give Moscow a powerful tool. Malkovich could undermine me by exposing the security failure.

Just because the blackmailers are in Moscow doesn't mean they couldn't sell the keyhole to other government embassies. The Chinese and the Iranians might be even more interested. They could move mirror shadows to coerce uncooperative neighbors.

Fauré responded as calmly as he could muster.

"We've got to close this keyhole immediately, in a way that no one except the blackmailers can use it ever again. Any sophisticated national government—China, Russia, India, Iran—could use the access to manipulate mirror shadows for its own short-term or long-term political advantage. Even being able to threaten such action could be effective.

"We don't even want them to think of the idea. I'm sure Director Wang told you how important it is that this intrusion never becomes public. We need to get to the blackmailers before they share their access or my documents."

"Yes, Wang told me. I agree you don't want to cut the blackmailers' only line of communication. We might even pay them some part of the money. Let me think about how to arrange that."

"If they contact me again, can I tell them that I'm working on getting the money? I don't know if they will believe me, but I want to hold out some hope to them."

"Yes, that's a good idea."

Cheng also recommended adding another layer of protection to MSTY and the Emergency Terminal: a voice recognition test for any oral communication from him. That way, instructions from any computer anywhere would necessitate approval by Fauré's computer-verified voice.

Fauré had another question for Cheng. "How soon can you leave for Moscow to see if we can catch the blackmailers?"

"It will take a few weeks to make the arrangements and get the proper clearances."

" I'd like you to take Jay Bhattachar and Kelly O'Rourke with you. They'll know a lot more by the time they return from Wuhan, and I'm sure you can use more eyes and ears."

Cheng shrugged. "I'm not sure it's so helpful to have amateurs along, but if you insist, I'll take them."

"Thank you."

After Cheng departed, Commander Fauré called Jay into his office, showed him a printout of the blackmail demand, and quickly outlined the recent events, including Cai's version of the facts and Natan's findings.

"I'm not confident SMS will treat these matters with the necessary urgency. We can't afford to have this story to make media news, certainly not before we have the answers. It would seriously damage SSPC's reputation, and it could give some governments ideas.

"I told Cai you would go to Wuhan to meet them in person. Your task is to determine if they are telling the truth and collect as much information as possible about CDI and NSSI. I hope you can accomplish the mission in three or four days there. If it turns out CDI is the blackmailer, tell them the deadline is impossible and get more time to respond.

"I understand this isn't your usual assignment, but I know you can handle it."

"I'll do my best, sir."

I would enjoy doing something more creative than preparing budget charts. If I can't be a fighter pilot, at least I can be an investigator for a week or two! I'll need to make arrangements for David and tell Sally, but I won't say no to the Commander or this opportunity.

The Commander continued, "Your mission will require a lot of detective work in a short time, so I'm sending Kelly O'Rourke along to assist you. She's capable and creative, and I'm sure you'll make a good team.

"Remember, we must catch these con men before they let the evil genie out of the bottle. The SSPC's survival depends on re-establishing MSTY's invincible status before anyone even starts to think about whether she could be compromised for someone's narrow advantage."

Jay struggled to hide his reaction. "Yes, sir. I'll inform her of your orders."

Will that work? Should I tell the Commander about my brief relationship with Kelly? What would that accomplish besides getting us both in trouble for unprofessional conduct?

And what difference would it make anyway? We'll carry out our mission just as we would otherwise. It's in both of our interests to do so. I just need to make sure Kelly understands it that way.

Chapter 18

Backtracking

THERE WERE OTHER LOOSE ends to tie up. Fauré needed to inform Ibrahim of his change of plans.

He certainly won't be happy, but I can't leave him in the dark.

"MSTY, please contact Director Mohamed Ibrahim. Ask him when he will be in New York, and invite him to meet with me for lunch, around noon, at his convenience."

"Do you want a reservation at the Millennium Hilton, sir?"

"No, I think someplace more out of the way would be better. Make it *The LCL Bar and Kitchen* in the Westin Grand Central. The quietest table they have."

"Yes, sir." Fifteen minutes later MSTY informed the Commander, "I have scheduled lunch for next Monday at 1300. Director Ibrahim will be coming by train from DC. He said he looks forward to seeing you."

"Excellent."

Ibrahim arrived late and seemed distracted. Fauré was waiting for him.

It doesn't look like he's coming from Washington, but that's not my business. I have my own problems to worry about.

"Good afternoon," Fauré began. "I appreciate your making time to meet with me. I want to let you know the status of the tourism matter.

"As you know, I explored the matter personally, studying the relevant maps and other information. MSTY satisfied me that fully solving the problem only involves a minor adjustment to a single object, and it would make no measurable difference to our mission.

"I had thought I could make an emergency adjustment immediately. But I've been reminded by others that our Operations Manual prescribes a formal public procedure before any such change. The procedure requires public notice and opportunity for comment, evaluation of the comments, and consultation with the Board before I approve."

Ibrahim lurched forward, interrupting, "Are you telling me you are reneging on your promise to make the change?"

Fauré responded carefully. "The obstacle is merely procedural. While I still believe the change is within my discretion, I've concluded it would be foolish to make this first change to the Master Plan without a transparent procedure.

"So I'm initiating that process. We'll release a Public Notice very soon. Others may respond by urging us to remedy perceived impacts on their facilities or other economic activities. Accommodating others with concerns similar to yours may have more significant adverse effects on the SSP mission. Any requests must be evaluated both separately and for cumulative impact.

"I don't need to tell you that the climate science purists will object to any changes because the experts designed the system to achieve the optimum effect and minimum harm globally.

"Those experts may have overlooked some surprising impacts of mirror shadows on various activities, but at that time and still today, no data is available on the subject. The outcome of the review process is not guaranteed.

"I'll do everything I can to expedite this process. I wish I could just push a button and ensure a favorable result. Unfortunately, the interested public will demand thorough scrutiny of this first change in the SSP's Master Plan, however desirable it seems to us.

"Your Board colleagues may also have opinions that I can't ignore. It's the best I can do, Ibrahim. I hope that's satisfactory."

Ibrahim leaned forward over the remains of his lunch.

"No, it isn't. Putting out a generic Public Notice will simply encourage others to insist that they deserve similar treatment when so far, they haven't given any thought to the subject.

"You told me before that you could resolve this problem quickly, yet now you plan to follow a formal procedure with no guarantee the SSPC will ever make the changes. The Maldives resorts discovered their problem on their own, and they need relief.

"Can't you just announce you have been informed of this one problem and fixed it, and leave the others for a separate Public Notice if anyone asks for it? Maybe no one will."

"I haven't seriously thought of doing that," Fauré prevaricated, "but I have recently learned that some other location operators actually do recognize this problem, so a Public Notice covering only one location would quickly lead to an outcry for review of other similar areas.

"Second, they and other observers would raise eyebrows if the Notice only identifies one location, and it has a close relationship with an SSPC Director. Once people start raising questions, I don't know what the media might allege or conclude."

Ibrahim was outraged. "I thought we had an understanding. Everything we have discussed is in the public interest and supports the SSPC's mission. Now you might never fix this economically damaging situation. Do you think that's fair?"

Fauré held his ground. "No, not entirely. Look, I wish I had a better solution. I've nothing to hide, and I assume you've nothing to hide. But I don't need to tell you that reputations are fragile, and once inquiries begin, they may even uncover unrelated embarrassing matters. I really think we would both be wise to avoid any appearance of favoritism that could be characterized as corrupt."

Fauré paused to give Ibrahim ample opportunity to respond, but Ibrahim sat in silence, frustrated. Finally, he spoke, shaking with emotion, "Your expert scientists made the original mistake, and the Maldives tourist resort industry and poor service workers will suffer grievously from it. You do what you feel you must do, and I'll do the same."

He rose and departed without saying another word. Fauré was dismayed at the intensity of Ibrahim's response.

It makes me wonder if he is genuinely innocent. Maybe money or promises did change hands. I could have Jay investigate, but right now, I have bigger fish to fry.

Fauré was also eager to know about the Malkovich committee's progress, but he didn't ask.

It's too risky. Expressing concern would just sharpen the tool in Ibrahim's hands. I can only hope Ibrahim doesn't join up with Malkovich out of spite.

∞∞∞

Ibrahim arrived at Wang Shu's apartment for dinner early that evening. They had long ago accepted the fact that no viable alternative existed for their relationship.

Ibrahim's wife Adeela suspected his frequent trips to New York meant he was seeing another woman, but she didn't raise the subject. Compared to living in Malé with a Foreign Minister husband who was always traveling or as a divorcé anywhere, she preferred her current life. She loved socializing in diplomatic circles in Washington, D.C. Their children benefitted from the city's excellent schools and America's best universities.

At dinner, Wang told Ibrahim some of what she learned from her conversation with Commander Fauré.

"I didn't whisper a word of what you already told me. I hope he can sort this out without entangling the SSPC in a scandal. That would be a tragic end to the years of work we have devoted to mitigating the pace of climate disruption using the Solar Shield."

Ibrahim wasn't worried about Fauré.

"We can count on him to get this threat under control. He's capable, and he has the most to lose."

"A scandal wouldn't help your reputation either. I assume no one paid you to intervene, but would people believe that? Is there any way you can help Fauré?"

"I don't think so. We'll just rely on your man Cheng to nip this matter in the bud."

They set the subject aside and returned to dinner, followed by lovemaking and a restless night's sleep. Ibrahim was more worried than he let on.

No money changed hands, but neither the UN nor World Bank would look kindly on me using my positions to rescue some struggling Maldives resorts. And there are other risks: questions about whether I was protecting Fauré from Malkovich; and of course, exposure of my relationship with Wang, which the media would love.

The Commander is even more vulnerable. I'm in no position to defend him if this story made the news. The Malkovich Committee or the Board could terminate him for mismanagement or failure to follow the procedures for amending the SSP Plan. It would do him no good to implicate me, but that doesn't mean he won't, either intentionally or inadvertently.

Part IV

Chapter 19

Mayhem in Wuhan

YAZEEN IMMEDIATELY BEGAN preparing for his mission to Wuhan. He needed various supplies for the physical aspect of his mission: A garden hose and a coping saw. Work clothes to protect him if he needed to scale walls, break glass, crawl on floors, or hide in unfamiliar places. Reliable wick materials for a Molotov Cocktail.

He found everything in his Harlem neighborhood. He cut the hose into a six-foot length for siphoning gasoline and two 18-inch sections for self-defense.

Flying to China and renting a car would require a passport, visa, and UID. His past connections with ISIS would make it too risky to use his US passport and New York UID. He wanted two complete sets of new documents from Ireland, each with a different name.

A few discreet inquiries led him to a "documents man" who made excellent forgeries of passports and UIDs. He also had blank Chinese visas with numbers already registered in the Chinese visa office—for a substantial fee.

Henceforth Yazeen could be Ahmed Alkoran or Mashad Anwar, as he wished. He also packed but would not use his South Sudanese passport in his real name, Yazeen Abdulla. A few experienced immigration clerks at the Beijing airport might recognize a fake Irish document, but Chinese hotel clerks and police inspectors were unlikely to spot them. Nevertheless, Yazeen was agitated as he finished packing his luggage.

There are so many opportunities for exposure. An inquisitive immigration or customs inspector could challenge my papers or the contents of my luggage. Forged documents alone would justify locking me up for years. If the Chinese discover my ISIS background, they might prosecute me as a terrorist—which would mean death, either fast or slow.

The US won't care what happens to me, and there's no US-China extradition treaty. I'll be stuck with Chinese justice. A spy, or even a double agent, at least has some national resources on his side. No one will come to rescue me.

Underlying these anxieties, Yazeen was deeply uncomfortable with his mission.

When I volunteered for ISIS, I was supporting a cause I believed in, and I was part of an army fighting another army, not a mercenary arsonist.

Jordan and Chris have promised to share part of their profits with me. But who knows if or how much they will set aside for me? What are my prospects for finding them if they renege?

But Yazeen had already committed himself.

Allah will dictate my fate. He will either see me captured in China or bring me safely back to a quiet life with my family and friends in Harlem.

His reverie was interrupted by a call from Chris.

"Yaz! You must hurry. The second call between Cai and Commander Fauré yesterday went worse for us than I could have foreseen.

"I expect SSPC and CDI will both be looking to trap us. We're counting on you to make CDI's records disappear. Meanwhile, we'll have dismantled NSSI. I'll make sure you get your share of whatever money is left. We won't forget you."

Yazeen tried to repress his skepticism. It was too late to change his mind. He had agreed to do the job and already received ₣300,000.

"I'm scheduled to leave tomorrow noon from JFK to Beijing, then to Wuhan. I'll work on destroying CDI's electronic records while I'm traveling. I should be able to finish everything and return in about four days. I'll let you know when I've finished, and I'll see you when I return."

"Inshallah!"

"Inshallah!"

ထထထ

Finally on the plane, Yazeen spent a few hours hacking CDI's computers to search for and delete all documents that mentioned NSSI. He found himself seated next to a talkative businessman from Dublin and took the opportunity to learn about the city where his documents said he lived.

As they left the plane, Yazeen realized he did not dare go through immigration or customs with his seatmate nearby. "I need to do some shopping here. It was nice meeting you. If I get to Dublin any time soon, I'll call."

He wandered off toward a jewelry store, letting the Irishman get went well ahead of him. At the back of the immigration line, he hoped the inspectors would be tired. Unfortunately, the shift changed just before he arrived at the counter.

The inspector looked through his otherwise empty passport with some surprise. He found the visa and took the time to check it against his online database of issued visas. To Yazeen's relief, it was still there.

The inspector slid the passport under the device that added the time, date, and place of entry into China, along with the scheduled time and date of departure.

Yazeen breathed a little more comfortably. He rode the shuttle to the newly-renovated Beijing Terminal 2 for the flight to Wuhan. Twenty-five hours after his departure from JFK, he checked in at the Leisure Hotel, not far from CDI's offices.

He immediately opened all his luggage, looking for signs that airport personnel had opened them for inspection. He was relieved to see the thin bits of tape placed across the interior closures were still in place.

He napped fitfully, then roused himself to explore the neighborhood as he walked to the CDI office building. On the way, using sign language, he bought a few inexpensive souvenirs that he would need later.

During the evening rush in the building's lobby, Yazeen entered and looked at the listing of companies and their offices. Fortunately, it was in both Chinese and English. CDI was listed on the ninth floor, just as and where expected. He also saw the building was old and showing its slipshod wood and fiberboard construction. It would burn quickly. Then he returned to his hotel for a leisurely dinner.

After dark, he returned to CDI's building and walked the block, the outside parking, and adjacent university campus woodlands, noting places to hide if necessary.

He watched the lights in the eighth- and ninth-floor offices go out, then tracked the night security guard's flashlight. He could see only one guard, who walked the floors intermittently. By midnight, Yazeen was confident CDI's and nearby offices were finally deserted.

I didn't come here to injure anyone, just destroy CDI's offices and physical ability to function.

He entered the building again long after dark, around 2300. "I have some things to deliver to the Hong Fujian Company on the ninth floor," he explained to the guard. The "delivery" in Yazeen's bag comprised the souvenirs he had bought the day before, along with two 1.5-liter Coca-Cola bottles. Yazeen held his breath as the guard poked through the bag with a stick.

"Not allowed. Can't go upstairs alone," the guard communicated in broken English and hand gestures. "Call—they come down for you."

"I know they are there. They said not to interrupt them. I will come right back down. 10 minutes."

The guard looked again at the trinkets, gave him a knowing smile, and said okay. As Yazeen rode the elevator, he became increasingly nervous.

I can't possibly finish in 10 minutes. The guard will come looking for me. I need to act quickly.

He knocked on the door of the Hong Fujian Company, hoping no one would answer. He timed the silence. *Ninety seconds—long enough.* He knocked on CDI's door and waited again. No answer there either.

He took out the first Coke bottle, placed it on the floor next to the CDI office, stretched out the wick and lit it. Then he raced down the stairs to the eighth floor, put the second coke bottle directly below CDI's office, and lit that fuse. He looked at his watch as he started down the stairs.

It's almost 12 minutes since I left the guard's desk, and it will be 15 minutes by the time I get back there. I can't afford to be in the building when the bottles explode. The explosion and fire will set off the building alarms. He'll detain me if he catches me.

Yazeen was still racing down when he heard the first explosion. Fortunately, the guard desk was unattended.

The guard had already boarded an elevator to find him. The explosions and fire automatically turned off his elevator on the fifth floor and opened the door.

Desperate to catch the intruder, he hurried down the stairs to the desk.

Yazeen ran toward the lobby door. The guard saw him and shouted, "Stop!" He ran to the desk and pressed the door lock switch. The explosions rattled him, and he took a few extra seconds to lock the exit doors.

Yazeen managed to escape.

In the CDI offices, Hua Luo Dan and his lover were sleeping on the floor in a back room when Yazeen knocked on the door. They didn't hear him. The roar of the explosions woke them.

They ran toward the only exit from the office. The hallway carpeting and wallboard and the wooden door were already in flames. They kicked down the door and dashed for the stairwell. They were overcome by a wall of smoke coming from the eighth floor.

The fire destroyed all of the ninth floor and most of the eighth floor. The investigators eventually found the remains of Hua and his girlfriend in the stairwell.

ꝏꝏꝏ

Yazeen returned to his hotel, slept soundly, and turned on the news when he awoke. The top local story was the dramatic fire that destroyed part of the old Dong Hu office building.

Fire officials had found two charred bodies, and the security guard had suffered severe burns fighting the blaze. He told his story truthfully to the fire investigators and was immediately charged with allowing an unauthorized, unaccompanied individual into the upper floors without identification.

Yazeen was distraught.

My mission was to disable the CDI office without injuring anyone. I had seen the lights go out hours earlier. I knocked on the door to be sure. But two people are dead. The police will be looking for me.

Yazeen threw away his contaminated clothes. He thought briefly about flying to some other destination where he would be harder to find and beyond extradition. But he wanted to see his wife and family and get the rest of his pay.

I don't trust Jordan and Chris to give me my money if I'm not physically present to demand it.

The best path was to check into a different hotel, stay in Wuhan another night, and skip the flight from Wuhan to Beijing. A fast train would get him there in 5 hours, so he didn't need to endure the 12-hour drive. The only nearby hotel was the Nice To Meet You Apartment Hotel. He took a room and slept, fitfully.

Chapter 20

Jay and Kelly, Investigators

JAY AND KELLY BOARDED THEIR flight to Beijing from JFK airport on February 23rd, unaware of the fire. Their conversation was limited to small talk and matters of logistics.

Jay spent the flight reviewing the timeline of events and the recordings and transcripts of MSTY's communications through the Emergency Terminal. He tried to construct a timeline that fit Cai's story that NSSI knew nothing about the realignments or the blackmail. Then he tried to create a version supporting the Commander's suspicion that Cai and CDI were themselves the ones responsible.

While both versions were possible, Jay concluded the evidence lent more support to Cai's explanation. Her questions and comments in the first conversation with Fauré were consistent with her legalistic disapproval of the Commander's Mirror 170 action and her suggestion she would overlook his lapse to protect the SSP—if he remedied the situation.

Moreover, computer analysis of Cai's baffled responses to the Commander's revelations—her tone of voice, emotion, and emphatic denial of extortion—pointed to an honest, innocent state of mind.

He also realized that while Cai might be completely innocent, other CDI employees might have used access to MSTY to pursue the nefarious schemes. He made a note to explore that possibility. Mostly, Jay was eager to learn everything possible about NSSI and the individuals who met with CDI and signed the contract directing them to hack MSTY.

Kelly's mind was in a completely different place. She had never traveled outside Ireland, Europe, and New York City. Traveling to China on a UN diplomatic passport for a serious investigation was a thrill.

At the same time, sitting beside Jay for 13 hours was too emotional to ignore. She longed to touch him, hold his hand, talk about their personal lives, more like honeymooners than SSPC investigators.

Jay showed her some of the transcripts and recordings of Cai Jin's conversations. Kelly pushed herself to concentrate on them in the hope of finding some clue that Jay had overlooked.

The last thing I want is for him to conclude that I'm a clueless female whose only professional use is to handle the travel records and chat up the people we are coming to interview. I want to be valuable in a more fundamental way. I don't need to worry about threatening his leadership; he must know I'm incapable of that. Nor would I want to try.

Kelly's conclusions after reviewing the recordings and transcripts coincided with Jay's. She was able to crystallize some of his thinking by focusing on additional bits of evidence showing Cai was innocent. "She never accused the Commander of lying, which would have been a natural way to cover her own lies, if there were any."

Kelly would have been happier had she been able to read Jay's emotions. He took care to bury them as completely as possible.

It's impossible to escape her beauty or my memories of that night. I'd love to be traveling to a romantic escape, or even a boring conference somewhere. But my first and only priority is the task at hand.

I also need to evaluate her performance objectively. How much can I rely on her intellect, resourcefulness, and loyalty right here and now? The Commander will want a thoughtful, objective report on her performance.

Arriving in Beijing, they were fascinated by the openness, beauty, and efficiency of the Beijing Capital Airport's International Terminal. Built to handle the millions of visitors coming for the 2008 Olympics, the terminal had employed new construction techniques that allowed for enormous, flexible open spaces under a massive flowing roof. Almost 40 years later, it was still aesthetically pleasing and capable of handling Beijing's vast number of travelers.

China needed that capacity this week, the tail end of the two-week Spring Festival or Chinese New Year when the urban Chinese population travels to their hometowns and farming villages, visiting family and the graves of ancestors. The country's transportation systems could never meet the demand during Spring Festival or Golden Week in the fall. Not even the years of the Covid-19 pandemic could stop this ritual for long. Despite the disruptive impact on production and bureaucratic functions, the government was unwilling to challenge these ancient patterns.

The cool weather, combined with the massive changeover to electric vehicles, the relocation of industry out of the city, and the ubiquitous progress toward working from home, gave Beijing more blue-sky days than its residents had experienced in the previous 60 years. Jay and Kelly were even able to see the mountains surrounding the city from the airport.

They changed terminals for their domestic flight to Wuhan, then took a self-driving taxi to the "Nice To Meet You Apartment Hotel," where Cai had reserved rooms for them.

It was more upscale than the kooky name suggested. A different local artist had decorated each guest room, and the décor varied from wildly psychedelic, to historical, to purely traditional. A video display on each floor showed all the room interiors.

Too exhausted by the 14 hours cooped up in planes, aggravated by the time change, they were ready for simple food and sleep. They made their plans for the coming day over a quick dinner and went to their rooms early, saying only "sleep well."

Once in his room, Jay contacted Cai at the URL she had provided. He was shocked by the news.

"You mean a fire destroyed your offices? And one of your employees died? Awful! I'm sure you must be deeply distressed."

"Yes. The attack was so unimaginable. We are a small organization. Our employees are devastated by the loss of Hua Luo Dan, our junior partner. We had no idea he ever met anyone there at night. The funeral rituals were this morning.

"The funeral service was very modest, as he had no spouse or children. His remains will be transported to his parents' hometown for cremation. The police have not yet identified the woman."

There was a tremor in Cai's voice as she struggled to talk about the death without losing control. She was still coming to grips with the grim reality.

Jay did his best to respond sympathetically, "I understand your pain completely. We will do our best to respect everyone's feelings. Is anything left of your office, or was everything destroyed?"

Jay feared the physical documents they came to see—contracts and checks, possibly with fingerprints and DNA traces, the layout of the CDI computer network, and possible evidence of hacking—might have been destroyed. Cai immediately realized what Jay was asking.

"The fire to our office destroyed everything. The attacker also seems to have erased all documents mentioning NSSI in our computer records in the cloud.

"Fortunately, in anticipation of your visit, I brought some key paper documents home to review and organize for you. I can bring them to your hotel in the morning."

"Thank you. The originals could be valuable. We might find fingerprints or even DNA traces on them that would help identify the NSSI people."

"You can meet with everyone in person in the morning. I'll ask the staff to come to your hotel."

Jay tried to be subtle in his response, but he needed to do things differently. "We don't want everyone to come at once. We'll talk to each of you individually, so if you can schedule each one for one-hour conversations, that would be helpful.

"You shouldn't attend any of these meetings yourself. It's better if each person is alone, in case their recollections differ. They may also mention sensitive facts that they would not want to reveal in front of you.

"Officer Kelly O'Rourke is accompanying me. We'll be recording the interviews, and we'll make transcripts for you if we learn anything that is even remotely interesting.

Cai was taken aback by the way Jay took charge and issued orders rather than discussing the arrangements.

"I guess we can do it that way, but I can tell you that everyone will be uncomfortable meeting alone with either of you. It's not the way we normally do things."

"We'll make every effort to encourage your staff to relax and tell us everything. I believe that's the best way to get the truth."

∞∞∞

Kelly awakened to the English-language local news and was horrified by what she saw of the fire in CDI's building. Suddenly the significance of their work in Wuhan submerged her personal musings about Jay. Not only was this effort significant, it could be dangerous. Two lives had already been lost.

It's time to get serious about what we're doing here. I need to focus my thoughts on it every waking minute. I want us both to come out of this alive!

They had already prepared for the CDI staff meetings—their names and work responsibilities, what to say, what to watch for, and what to avoid.

They donned their distinctive sky-blue SSPC uniforms with silver trim in preparation for the staff interviews and went to the hotel dining room for breakfast. It was a bustle of activity, designed for Chinese guests.

The dining room décor seemed a little tired, with faded paint, old tablecloths, and artificial flower centerpieces. Most tables were large and filled with families on vacation, tour groups, or businesspeople.

The generous buffet included fried noodles, hard-boiled eggs, tofu, rice with bits of egg and vegetables, congee with tiny, dried fish and other condiments, marinated fish, pork and vegetable dumplings, lots of fruit, and watermelon and tomatoes for dessert. Almost no recognizable cuts of chicken or beef.

The ubiquitous steamed "green vegetable" could be anything, from bok choy to spinach, depending on availability. Carafes of tea and coffee were warm but not hot enough for Western tastes. The aromas from the sesame and palm oils were intense and distinctive, unlike anything Kelly had ever experienced.

Jay, who had lived in Beijing for a year and knew Chinese food, quickly filled his plate. Kelly had no idea where to begin. She followed Jay, determined to try everything he chose. Jay pointed out the congee and the tiny whole dried fish, chopped vegetables, and dried pepper to add to it. She managed to down most of the food on her plate but abandoned a few items after a small taste.

Jay found a small table near the wall where they could see the whole room. As Kelly surveyed the scene, a man across the room caught her attention. He was by himself, no longer eating, but drinking coffee and reading an English-language newspaper. He appeared to be Middle Eastern and not in any hurry.

When he glanced up, he saw Jay and Kelly in uniform. He quickly folded his newspaper and slipped out of the room, taking the route farthest from their table.

Kelly noted his rapid movement. *What's that about? I'll mention it to Jay, but not here.*

When they finished eating and walked to their rooms, Kelly followed Jay into his room. "Did you notice the man sitting by himself, reading the English-language newspaper? He looked foreign, yet he seemed to be in no hurry to do anything—until he noticed us in our uniforms. Then he left hastily, avoiding our side of the dining room."

"I did notice his unusual behavior. But remember, this is a city of 15 million people, with millions of visitors every year from around the world. We haven't got time for distractions."

Kelly was disappointed in Jay's dismissive response, but she pursued the matter.

"Let me see what the desk clerk will tell me. Maybe he'll be impressed enough by my uniform to share some information."

Noticing Kelly's hurt feelings, Jay backtracked. "Okay. I guess there's no harm in asking. You might learn something."

Kelly approached the young man working at the receptionist desk.

"I'm Officer Kelly O'Rourke from the United Nations. I think I met you yesterday when I checked in. I'm sorry if I wasn't very friendly. We were exhausted from traveling from New York via Beijing."

Handing him her SSPC ID, she continued, "I'm an investigator from the Space Shield Command. Officer Bhattachar and I are in Wuhan to investigate a crime with international significance. I am hoping you can tell me something about one of your guests."

The clerk was torn. He had been trained from childhood to respect the authority of people in uniform, and he wanted to help. But the hotel management's instructions were clear. "I'm not supposed to share any guest's files."

Kelly tried bluffing. "I could get a court order to obtain the file, but that would take more time than we have, and the publicity might reflect badly on your hotel. I just want to see a suspicious guest's file. Could you please help me?"

Kelly's face showed her unhappiness. She gave no indication she accepted his answer. The psychological pressure on the clerk was unbearable.

"I can pass you his electronic file, but you can't tell anyone that you saw it or got it from me."

"Of course not. The person I'm interested in was at breakfast this morning. I don't know what his passport says, but he is not Chinese—probably from an Arab country. Do you know who I mean?"

"He just checked out this morning, saying something about getting to the train station. He's Irish, according to his passport."

Kelly's eyes opened wide. "Really! I'm Irish! I'm sorry I didn't have a chance to chat with him. Just send me what you have. That would be wonderful!"

Kelly gave the clerk her most appreciative smile and went back to her room. The clerk's email arrived immediately, including images of his Irish passport, UID, and Chinese visa.

Kelly studied the images and eagerly reported her conclusions to Jay. "The desk clerks may not have recognized it, but I think the Irish documents are fake. The color and the font don't match my Irish passport or UID. This guy may or may not be relevant to our case, but we should certainly report him to the Chinese government authorities."

Jay was less enthusiastic. "Please keep in mind we're not even authorized UN investigators or police officers. I'll send this material to Inspector Cheng and tell him you suspect forgeries. He can take it from there. We have other work to do."

ꝏꝏꝏ

Yazeen tried to relax on the train to Beijing, but without much success. Seven hours later, he was standing around the Beijing Capital Airport. He felt so nervous he wondered if he looked suspicious from that fact alone. Moreover, even though Yazeen's visa gave him another twenty days, the passport entry stamp said he was scheduled to fly out the previous day. As the officer stared at the computer record, Yazeen feared that he would realize the documents were forged.

He struggled to explain his schedule change to the immigration officer. "My business negotiations took more time than I expected. The other side asked for another big concession just when I thought we had a deal.

"What is the nature of your business?"

"We buy inexpensive, reusable, dishwasher-safe bamboo plates for restaurants, so they don't generate so much waste."

"Good for the environment, yes?"

"Definitely. The plates cost a little more, but even if they are only reused two or three times, it significantly reduces environmental waste."

The officer smiled, happy to know China was helping solve the global waste problem mentioned in the news every month. Fortunately for Yazeen, the airport was busy, and the clerk saw no harm in letting him leave a day later than his original tickets provided.

∞∞∞

At 900, Jay and Kelly proceeded to the hotel's Conference Room B to interview the five CDI staff members.

Jay and Kelly were appropriately somber and sympathetic as they began their inquiries. They were eager to learn if any of them had contacts with NSSI and whether the woman who died with Hua could possibly have been a source of inside information about CDI and MSTY.

Initially, each one disclaimed any knowledge of the woman's identity or her relationship to Hua or NSSI. Kelly pursued the matter more obliquely. She prompted them to look at their electronic photos and emails. Their photos quickly led to more information from staff members who had initially recalled nothing in their depressed state of mind.

Hua had brought a guest to some recent staff social gatherings. Photos and videos from the events revealed her appearance and approximate age.

He probably met her when they both worked at the Air Force Computer Command Center. Nothing suggested any connection with NSSI or any meaningful knowledge of details of Hua's work.

Other responses revealed that CDI had not worried much about safeguarding its own network. NSSI could have tapped CDI's system without much difficulty. With a continuing hack, they could have instantly learned about the SSPC Emergency Terminal and cloned it for their own purposes.

Jay reported their results to Commander Fauré, who passed them along to Inspector Cheng. Then Jay and Kelly arranged to begin flying home in the morning.

Chapter 21

A Wuhan Evening

IT HAD BEEN ANOTHER LONG day, but Jay and Kelly had accomplished everything they had hoped for in Wuhan. Kelly was also pleased with her substantial contribution, at least in her own judgment. She also felt Jay was treating her as a partner, not merely a clerk. Feeling more self-assured, she took a chance with Jay.

"Can I suggest we have dinner in a nice restaurant? We have plenty of time, and we've spent practically nothing on food. Our expense account can take it."

"I suppose we can afford to enjoy a first-class dinner. Who knows we might get to eat authentic Chinese food in China?"

They asked for a good restaurant nearby. Relying on their Western appearance, the concierge suggested the Burger King and the McDonald's, both within walking distance. When Jay clarified that they wanted authentic Chinese food, the concierge smiled proudly.

"The absolute best Chinese restaurant is Kàng Lóng Tàizǐ Jiǔ Xuān, which means Kang Long Prince

Restaurant. It's about 30 minutes away by taxi, but it's well worth the trip.

He scribbled something on a small piece of paper.

"Here's the address in Chinese for the taxi driver, and take a hotel card so you will have our address in Chinese for your return."

Jay and Kelly thanked him for what they hoped would be a distinctive experience. They changed out of their uniforms into less conspicuous, more comfortable clothes. The taxi driver studied the paper and recognized 亢龙太子酒轩.

The restaurant was pleasantly appointed, though more brightly lit than Kelly had hoped. The menu was bewilderingly elaborate, but Jay solved that problem by asking in Chinese for the chef's best meal for two. He also ordered an excellent Australian wine.

Kelly offered a humorous toast "to our first successful collaboration as intrepid investigators for the UNSSP."

Jay responded with a more serious comment. "I wondered how this trip would go from several angles when the Commander paired us for it. I'm pleased to say our results are as much as I could have hoped.

"You have been a full partner in achieving this result. You have been observant, cooperative, and creative. And the Commander will know my conclusions."

Kelly was in heaven. The praise was exactly what she needed. Prudence suggested resting on her laurels, but Jay's recognition was too powerful to manage according to the rules. She couldn't erase that one night with him in her apartment. So she stopped trying.

The multi-course meal that followed was excellent, though cooked and spiced in ways neither had ever experienced before: hot-sour soup, snails larger than they had ever seen, "green vegetable," crispy noodles with vegetables, broiled whole lobster, mu-shu pork with Mandarin pancakes, and a choice of watermelon or Western pastry for dessert.

They returned to the hotel at an early hour by New York standards, both wide awake and pleasantly buzzed from the wine. They stopped to watch the guest room art video and pointed out the décor of their respective rooms.

When they arrived at her door, Jay said good night and turned to walk away. But Kelly refused to let this chance get away. She put her hand on his arm. Her words were even more explicit.

"Jay, earlier this evening, you said something like, 'Who knows when another opportunity like this might arise again?' Can't we make a China exception? I have no ulterior motive, and I'll never do anything to hurt you.

"I was attracted to you before we came here, and that attraction to you has grown stronger every minute we have been working together. Please, let's not pass up this moment!"

Jay was transfixed. The rules were clear. They were on official travel. No exceptions applied. He had already told Kelly he would never make this mistake again.

But he could not get "No" out of his mouth.

After a moment of paralyzed silence, he kissed her. She opened the door to her room. No lingering doubt or anxious resistance stood in the way. Neither had dared expect this to happen, but both had hoped it would.

Two hours later, Jay tried to reconstruct his defenses. "Please remember, Kelly, that you asked for a 'China exception.' This can't happen at home."

Kelly nodded her head. "I understand that. But it was wonderful. Thank you for this moment." Jay knew he was already unavoidably in her control if Kelly chose to use it. He'd already spilled that milk.

Kelly swore an oath to herself. *He fears the power I have over him and feels that threat, no matter how much he wants me. I will never use it to his disadvantage, no matter how he may distance himself from me or treat me in the future.*

I need to find a way to show that reality to him. I asked him for our affair, and he gave me what I asked for despite his fear. It was an expression of trust I must keep earning every day.

In the morning, they ate breakfast in the hotel dining room, packed, and departed for the airport, both trying to behave as if nothing unusual had happened in the last 12 hours. Their conversations were all business; they never came close to touching.

Nevertheless, the reality was impossible to ignore. The intensity of Jay's desire for her would no doubt fade when they were back at home. But they both knew that if they were ever alone together, that chemistry would emerge.

Chapter 22

Harlem Confrontation

YAZEEN ARRIVED HOME safely but still shaken by the deaths of the two innocent people. As he passed the next few days with friends and family, he slowly calmed down. He settled into his routine over the next few days. The risk of being tied to the events in Wuhan seemed increasingly remote.

He had reported his success to Jordan and Chris by email from Wuhan without mentioning the deaths. He asked for the rest of his money. Chris put him off, saying there were still questions about how much money was left.

Two days later, Chris consulted with Jordan and wired another ₣200,000 to Yazeen. It was only about 25% of what he had expected. Yazeen immediately wired the funds to an account in the name of his wife's payday loan company, where it would be beyond Chris's reach. He no longer trusted anything Chris told him.

The next day Yazeen went to the NSSI's office space. It was in a drab, cavernous dark corner on the second floor of an industrial warehouse at 2333 12th Avenue in West Harlem. The ancient building was wedged between 12th Avenue under Riverside Drive to the east, and to the west the elevated Henry Hudson Parkway, some railroad tracks, and the north end of the Hudson River Greenway.

Yazeen was dismayed to discover that the space was already almost empty: no staff, only scraps of equipment, and only a few sticks of abandoned office furniture. Most important, Jordan and Chris were gone.

Yazeen got an update from the landlord's agent, Shoshana Jacobs. "NSSI just evaporated overnight. Jordan and Chris left no contact information. I'm already looking for a replacement tenant."

Yazeen told Jacobs he was an employee of NSSI who had just returned from overseas and didn't know about the management's plans.

"I hope to find a new job as a computer programmer in a short time. I don't want to frighten my family with news that I'm suddenly unemployed. Would it be possible for me to continue to use the office for a few weeks or until you find a new tenant?"

Jacobs considered the idea. Having a person in the space would have advantages. "I guess that will be okay if you keep the premises clean, keep the rats out, and don't let anyone else in."

"Certainly." They put their hands on their hearts to signal agreement. Handshakes between strangers had largely disappeared among New Yorkers seared by the Covid-19 pandemic fifteen years before.

∞∞∞

Jordan, now "Charles Morgan," and Chris, now "Jomo Kahinde," had flown to Moscow three days after they closed the NSSI office, traveling on newly-acquired forged passports and matching visas.

They had paid Yazeen what they considered a fair sum for his few days in Wuhan. They had already given generous severance pay to each former NSSI employee. Then they asked their bank, FirstWorld Bank of Capetown, to wire the entire ₣ 12,000,000 of NSSI funds to the International Commercial Bank of Juba in Juba, South Sudan (ICB Juba). FirstWorld wired the funds in smaller amounts to numerous ICB Juba accounts over the next two weeks to avoid various reporting requirements.

Over their first few weeks in Moscow, they contacted a few similarly situated expats to learn the ropes of living anonymously in Russia. They invested half of their funds in legitimate Russian businesses, enough to make them eligible for permanent residency as investors. They had sufficient resources left over to support a comfortable life in Moscow. It was time to lay low, perhaps for the indefinite future.

Chris rented a pleasant apartment near Pushkin Square, across from the green space that once held a wall protecting ancient Moscow. Jordan purchased a large townhouse in a secure suburban gated community.

∞∞∞

Twenty-four hours after their unforgettable dinner in Wuhan, Jay and Kelly arrived back in New York. Both were acutely aware that the "China exception" could no longer apply. They were back at SSPC and had serious work to do.

After debriefing Commander Fauré and Inspector Cheng, they volunteered to search for Jordan and Chris in Harlem. Cheng reluctantly agreed, insisting that they update him daily on their progress or need for backup. He was too busy with other matters to join them.

While the handwriting and DNA labs were doing their work, Jay and Kelly had only the NSSI address and two names to guide their search. The address didn't seem likely to be much help. It led them to the rundown industrial warehouse.

Jay and Kelly showed their SSPC credentials to the building manager, Ms. Jacobs. She told them NSSI had abandoned the space seven days before. She was already looking for a new tenant.

"You're welcome to talk to the security guards, enter the space, take anything you find, and talk with anyone there. I'm always happy to work with the police. I need their protection; there are too many potential criminals in this neighborhood."

She emailed them the electronic form lease signed by NSSI's representatives, Jordan Milhaus and Christopher Kangata. "They paid automatically by bank transfer, but I don't expect anything for the most recent month's rent. That's what usually happens when a business suddenly closes." The automatic payment documents showed a bank account at FirstWorld Bank.

Jay and Kelly waited for the shift change so they could talk with both the day and night security guards. The guards showed them a list of NSSI's employees.

Mac, the day guard, explained, "This log lists everyone who came here regularly. There's one employee still hanging around the office. You might want to talk to him. He says he's looking for another job. His name is Ammar Abdulla."

At this point Santiago, the night guard, jumped into the conversation. "That's the name he gave us when he arrived here last week, but I'm pretty sure he used to call himself Yazeen something or other. He was only here once in a while, and he wasn't here when everyone came to clean out the office.

"He showed us an Irish passport and UID with that name on it last week. I was surprised to see Irish citizenship. He says he's a former NSSI employee. I'm not sure whether we still have the UID of the Yazeen guy. If we do, it would be in the files here.

"I'm not sure he's the same guy—these Middle Easterners all look alike to me, and it's not our problem. We just need a name and UID for the files.

"But he sure looks familiar."

Kelly's eyes opened wide. She looked at Jay, who nodded. She started to say something but caught herself. *Don't say anything in front of the guards.*

Jay turned to Santiago. "So when is he usually here?"

"During the day."

"Do you think he's here now?"

"Let me check," Santiago replied, looking at the computer. "It says he is, but we don't always get it right."

"Can I go up and take a look? He may be able to tell us something about NSSI's business."

"Sure. I'll take you up there."

Jay turned to Kelly. Her eyes begged to come along. "Please wait here and see if you and Mac can find anything about Yazeen in the old logs. I don't think we'll take very long. If he's here, I don't want to frighten him with a crowd. If he's willing to talk, I'll send the guard down for you."

As they rode the front elevator to the second floor, Santiago, a retired NYPD cop, unsnapped the protective cover on his holster. They walked to the NSSI office. Jay let Santiago take the lead, and he knocked on the door.

A voice from inside called, "Who is it?"

"It's Santiago. I've got someone here who says NSSI owes him some money for computer equipment. He'd like to talk to you." Jay smiled at Santiago's creative response.

Yazeen shuffled some things on his desk as he responded, "Okay, come on in."

They entered the room, which was bare except for a single small desk and worn-out chair. Yazeen was standing.

"Hi. We've met before. I'm Santiago, the night security guard. This is . . ."

"Sanjay Bhattachar. It looks like NSSI left nothing behind, including the leased computers. Where is everybody?"

Yazeen answered slowly, arranging his story in his head as he talked. "I don't know. I was traveling for a few days, and when I came back, the boss informed me that the company had closed. Maybe he told the staff they could take their computers with them.

"I don't know where the boss went. If you find him, I'd like to talk with him about my overdue pay."

"Where would you suggest we look?"

"I wish I knew. I tried his apartment, but the concierge said he had moved out. His name was Jordan Milhaus. Sounded very British to me."

Santiago interrupted. "Do you have any identification with you? I looked through our records, and we don't have a copy of your ID. I guess the copier was broken, or Mac would have made a copy."

"Sure," he answered, handing over his Irish passport and UID.

Santiago examined them. "Ammar Abdulla. Good. I'll just take them downstairs, make copies, and bring them right back up. By the way, are you related to someone named Yazeen, who worked here for a while? He looked a lot like you."

Suddenly Yazeen realized the precariousness of his situation. These visitors were more interested in him than in missing computers. Entering the US on a false passport would be enough to put him in jail for years, whether or not they could connect him to the events in Wuhan. And Jay looked familiar somehow.

"Yazeen? I don't know anyone by that name. Look, if you are searching for missing computers, you can see there aren't any here. If you are looking for this Yazeen person and want to question me about him, I think you need a warrant. You haven't shown me any identification at all. I have other matters to attend to, including dinner with my family. So if you don't mind, I'm going to leave."

As he spoke, Yazeen put his hand under the materials on his desk and gripped his new Beretta M9B2.

Santiago, seeing Yazeen's right hand resting on the desk, whispered, "Please put both hands in the air where I can see them. I don't want any surprises."

Yazeen pulled the gun from the papers and pointed it in the air. "I don't think you heard me. You have no basis for holding me here, and I am going home. Please step aside and let me go out the door, and don't try to follow me."

He picked up his briefcase and walked quickly toward the door. Standing in the doorway, he turned and lowered his gun. Santiago had already drawn his own M&P 9mm LE.

Yazeen fired a shot, hitting Jay's leg and knocking him to the ground. Santiago expertly shot Yazeen in the right shoulder. The gun fell from Yazeen's hand. He staggered out the door and ran to the rear elevator, looking over his shoulder for Santiago.

Santiago turned his first attention to Jay. He was quickly satisfied that Jay was only slightly injured, then ran to pursue Yazeen. He was already gone. Santiago returned to attend to Jay's wound.

Kelly heard the gunshots. She was horrified at the thought that Jay might be injured. *He can't die now, when I've finally found someone I love. I need him!*

She ran to the front elevator, suffered through the agonizingly slow ascent, and rushed to the NSSI office. Jay was still lying on the floor. Seeing her distress, Santiago tried to reassure her. "The bullet grazed him. I don't think it's in his leg. He may need some stitches, but he'll be fine."

Kelly burst into tears, then quickly collected herself and called an ambulance. *This is no time to fall apart. I can do that later, when he's safely in the hands of a doctor. I'm not even sure he's conscious right now.*

Thirty minutes later, doctors at Sinai Hospital were suturing Jay's leg. Santiago was mistaken about the bullet, which the doctor removed, but it had not hit the bone. His fall had been soft; he showed no sign of a concussion. His condition was not critical.

∞∞∞

Downstairs, Yazeen quietly made his way to the freight loading dock at the back of the building. Once outside, he turned south and ducked into the adjacent alley.

He initially thought he would cross the tracks and make his way to the Greenway, where he could disappear among the evening's joggers. But his shoulder was bleeding too much. He needed an emergency room immediately.

Yazeen called a robotaxi to avoid any unpleasant questions. It took him past the Apollo Theater and then up Lennox to the NYC Health+ Hospital at 137th. His wound was critical, but once the doctors sutured and bandaged it, he was allowed to depart.

Twelve hours later, wearing a new shirt and suit, he boarded a flight to Addis Ababa, using his real South Sudan passport with his real name, Yazeen Abdulla. From Addis, two more flights—first to Nairobi, Kenya, then to Juba, the South Sudan capital. No visa was necessary when Yazeen arrived home from his decades-long odyssey.

Over the next three weeks, Yazeen transferred most of the money in his wife's business account to a new account at the ICB Juba. He set up a computer business to keep himself busy and cover the true source of his comfortable income.

He wondered if anyone would or could connect the dots or even try to pursue him. He didn't realize how easy it had become to trace international funds transfers after the ratification of the 2029 *Protocol on Government Access to Financial Records of Transnational Fund Transfers by Banks and Securities Firms.*

That Protocol strengthened the money-laundering provisions of the 2000 *United Nations Convention against Transnational Organized Crime.* After 2029, all international transfers over ₣ 25,000 were automatically reported to the IMF.

Chapter 23

Tracing the Cash

IN A WEEK, JAY WAS HOBBLING with the help of a leg brace and working vigorously at his prescribed physical therapy. Kelly was with him whenever he was not in treatment, going over what they had learned and planning the next steps. She was relieved to see him alive, though she dare not touch him. She struggled to concentrate on the work at hand.

The next step was straightforward. Follow the money. NSSI banked at the New York City branch of FirstWorld Bank, which primarily served US non-citizen residents.

"I can do that," she asserted, "I've dealt with bank officers before. They don't carry guns."

Jay hesitated to let Kelly go to the bank alone, but he was not yet ready to test his ability to walk unassisted. He reluctantly agreed.

At the bank, she flashed her brightest smile and SSPC credentials and got an immediate meeting with the bank president, Isaac Swerdling. In response to her request to see the entire NSSI account records, he raised the usual customer secrecy objections.

But he relented when confronted with the information that SMS was investigating a set of crimes involving murder as well as cybersecurity. Kelly also implied that SMS was not interested in whether FirstWorld Bank had reported all international transfers over ₣ 25,000, but that could change if Swerdling was uncooperative.

Kelly's examination of the NSSI account showed everything she had hoped to learn. It was still open, but nearly all the several million ₣ had been transferred abroad two weeks earlier, in multiple transactions under ₣ 25,000.

The transfers went to multiple accounts at ICB Juba. Enough funds remained to cover the outstanding office rent and other miscellaneous matters, leaving a few thousand ₣ to keep the account active. Other transfers included a domestic payment of ₣ 300,000 to "Yazeen Abdulla." Kelly was delighted.

Now we know where to find the money, and that's where Jordan and Chris will be. We're about to wrap up this case for Inspector Cheng. I wonder if he would have been able to get Swerdling to give up the records as quickly as I did.

Kelly reported to Jay after his physical therapy session. "I found exactly what we wanted to know. Three weeks ago, NSSI transferred ₣ 12,000,000 from its account in FirstWorld Bank to numerous ICB Juba accounts. So now we know where to find Jordan and Chris and their ill-gotten gains."

"Not so fast," Jay cautioned. "We don't know if they went to Juba themselves, or even if the money is still there. Why don't you check to see if either of them has flown anywhere this month?

"For all we know, they put ₣100,000 directly into their own pockets for living expenses and stayed right here in New York. Or perhaps they outfitted themselves with completely new identities and went elsewhere."

Kelly looked deeply embarrassed.

I should have thought through all the possibilities more carefully instead of jumping on the first scenario that came to mind.

Trying to save face, she reiterated her initial conclusion with even more confidence. "Maybe, but I think the best course is for me to take the next plane to Juba and talk to ICB Juba."

"Talk with Cheng first to see if they flew to Juba or anywhere else. And check with the IMF Unlawful Funds Transfers Office to see what they have on FirstWorld Bank and ICB Juba. Cheng knows tricks we don't."

"Okay. I'll see what I can learn. Talk to you tomorrow."

Kelly met with Inspector Cheng in the morning. She shared the documents she obtained from President Swerdling at FirstWorld Bank. She proudly mentioned her hint about willingness not to prosecute FirstWorld for money-laundering if he turned over the records.

"Jay suggested I talk with you about a few loose ends before I head off to Juba. Can you help me find out if

Jordan or Chris left the country since they closed NSSI and wired the funds to Juba?

"Jay also thought you might also be able to find out whether the money is still at ICB Juba—I guess from the IMF unit that watches for illegal transfers?"

Cheng's face turned to a scowl. "You weren't authorized to make any promises to Swerdling or anyone else, explicit or implicit. SMS has been watching FirstWorld Bank's operations for some time in the hope of catching some illegal transactions we can document.

"Now it will be awkward to try to prosecute them on any illegal transfers before you met with him. He'll say you promised him immunity if he gave you these documents. This case would have been an excellent opportunity to put him out of business. Now we'll need to start over."

Kelly blanched. "I hadn't realized they were under surveillance. I'm sorry."

"I know. You're new at this. We have lots of people trying to enforce the 2029 Convention. I don't know myself what their next target is. I just happen to know about this one because I worked on the case. But next time, let me know before you make any commitments to anyone.

"Now, you want to know if Jordan or Chris has left the country. And whether the money is still in Juba. I can probably have some answers for you tomorrow. Come back and see me at the end of the day."

Kelly thanked Cheng profusely and apologized for her error. To Jay, she simply reported that she had asked his help, and he told her to come back tomorrow.

No need to advertise my mistakes. Maybe Cheng won't get around to telling Jay or putting a note in my file. I hope he was exaggerating for effect.

Kelly eagerly appeared at Cheng's office at 1600 the next day. He was pleased to see her.

"Here's what I learned. It's even more than you requested. First, Jordan and Chris appear to have left the US a day or two after the fire at CDI's office, which they probably learned about, including the resulting deaths. The Kennedy International Airport facial recognition system identified them. They flew as "Charles Morgan" and "Jomo Kahinde," using forged passports and visas, along with other false identification. Their flight went to Moscow. We have reason to believe they are still there.

"Second, Jordan and Chris withdrew their money from ICB Juba shortly after arriving in Moscow. I don't know yet where they have transferred the ₣12,000,000 since then, but if any of them were international transfers over ₣25,000, the IMF has the records.

"Our suspects know enough to split the funds into multiple pieces either immediately or after some further laundering. They could have put it in various banks, invested in local businesses, or used it for living expenses or bribes where necessary. In that case, we will have a harder time tracking it. But you can save yourself the trip to Juba, which I can assure you would not be pleasant.

"Yazeen might still be there. He sent ₣200,000 and all the funds in his wife's business accounts to ICB Juba. He used a real South Sudan passport with the name Yazeen Abdulla to board a flight to Addis Ababa, then to Juba via Nairobi. His use of his real documents suggests he may intend to stay there.

"His wife left New York a few days later with the children, which indicates that she might be joining him in Juba.

"By the way, Yazeen was once a terrorist fighting for ISIS and Hezbollah. He defected to Iraq in 2023 and was given his freedom in exchange for valuable information about Hezbollah and Iranian influences.

"The United States still considers him suspicious. But it has chosen not to arrest him in light of the Iraqi government's promise to him and his exemplary behavior since coming here."

Kelly suppressed a "Wow!" She didn't want to say anything that would mark her as a complete neophyte, but her wide-eyed look gave her away.

"Thank you. That's a lot of valuable information. I still think it makes sense to pursue Yazeen Abdulla in Juba.

"He's almost certainly an accomplice to Jordan and Chris's fraudulent claims to be contractors for the SSPC, and to Chris's claim to be an SSPC employee, and maybe the attempted extortion of Commander Fauré.

"And we have reason to believe he was responsible for the fire and deaths at the CDI office. NSSI may have also paid him for this death and destruction. So he was unquestionably more than a bystander to all this.

"Moreover, he may know more about where Jordan and Chris are. He turned on former leaders once before, and maybe he'll do it again. He could be a crucial witness against Jordan and Chris if we're ever able to capture them."

Cheng paused before replying. "I appreciate your enthusiasm. Capturing any or all of these criminals is a worthwhile endeavor that sets an example for others who might try to impersonate UN personnel.

"But you and Jay are not trained professionals, and I cannot recommend that you pursue any of these people. We already know Yazeen carries a pistol and is capable of murder, especially to protect himself and his family. Jordan and Chris appear to be equally ruthless. Why don't you leave the rest of the investigation to us?"

Kelly was unwilling to give up on pursuing the man who shot Jay. She would gain nothing by arguing with Cheng, but that didn't mean she would follow his advice.

"I appreciate what you are saying. I know you will do everything you can to bring these criminals to justice.

"Right now, I'm obligated to follow Jay's instructions. I'll see how he and Commander Fauré wish to proceed."

Cheng was not happy with this response, but he could not tell Kelly to disregard her superiors. He would talk with them.

Kelly thanked Cheng again and quickly departed. She already knew what she wanted to do—if Jay would let her. But the decision was not Jay's, either.

Commander Fauré, already advised by Cheng, was unequivocal. "No, Jay, Kelly is not to go to Juba. It's a dangerous place for anyone, let alone a female with no background in the civil war there or serious training in how to protect herself in a violence-prone city."

Kelly was disappointed. *The Irish Air Force trained me for battle zones. It's just bias against women.*

But I have to admit that the only urban areas I've experienced are Dublin and Manhattan's Upper East Side. Maybe they are right. Going to Juba alone could be hazardous.

Unwilling to abandon the pursuit, she reviewed the IMF's Illegal Transfers records. She found Yazeen's accounts but no illegal transfers. The local UN officers obtained the last two months' account activity from ICB Juba. Examining them revealed current use of the accounts to pay local bills, which suggested that Yazeen was still in Juba.

Then she examined Jordan's and Chris's account records. She found physical and electronic addresses of fund recipients, many of them Russian businesses. The individual details were unexciting, but taken together, she thought they painted a picture.

She eagerly told Jay and Cheng the results of her search into the IMF and ICB Juba records. Although the individual transfers from FirstWorld Bank were less than ₣ 25,000, FirstWorld was already under surveillance, and the number of transactions was so large that the IMF computers had already flagged them for review.

Cheng appreciated her commitment to the tedious research, even after he had killed her dream of a trip to Juba.

"Your analysis of these records will be decisive. I can persuade the UN force in Juba to find and arrest Yazeen on the strength of this information. Then we'll see if we can bring him to justice, either there or in the US.

"You might eventually get a trip to Juba to assist in the prosecution, but if so, you will have proper credentials and a UN bodyguard."

The UN did eventually capture Yazeen and persuaded South Sudan to bring legal proceedings against him. It might be many months before the local courts issued a final judgment, but Kelly and Jay had their first concrete success as UN investigators.

Part V

Chapter 24

Searching For The Big Fish

JORDAN AND CHRIS WERE MOST likely in Moscow, the second largest capital in Europe and the eleventh largest capital city on Earth—over 12 million official residents plus an unknown number of "temporary" foreign workers, legal and illegal foreign visitors, students, and immigrants. Over 250,000 are long-term expats, ranging from career diplomats and corporate executives to hustlers at every level trying to get rich quick. The city continues to grow despite Russia's declining total population.

Russia has no extradition treaty with the US. It does not allow extradition of its citizens, except by individual agreement. With the funds at their disposal, Jordan and Chris acquired documents that made them "qualified foreign investors." They hoped this status would protect them from extradition or deportation.

However, the US and Russia are among the 190 parties to the United Nations Convention Against Transnational Organized Crime, which came into effect in 2003 and directs all parties to cooperate in extraditing transnational criminals.

The UN's authority to demand extradition is limited to individuals accused of war crimes and crimes against humanity. It relies on national laws to protect its operations from ordinary crimes. Federal or New York State prosecutors must initiate any legal action in the US.

Cheng's IT support staff had already begun methodically collecting all the information they could from the airlines and banks that Jordan and Chris were known to have used. They looked for aliases and addresses, current business investments, email addresses, mobile numbers, and other data that could lead to their apprehension.

With Kelly's additional information, they were able to assemble a coherent picture of the physical and financial lives of "Charles Morgan" and "Jomo Kahinde" that would be crucial to show their illegal conduct.

But Cheng did not expect Moscow officials to be very cooperative in this pursuit.

These two alleged white-collar criminals haven't committed any offense against Russia. Proving a connection to the deadly fire in Wuhan would be problematic at best. Even winning an abstract "cybercrime" case attacking the UN would do little to strengthen the police or prosecutors' resumes.

The police and prosecutors faced other potential risks. Which influential people might have helped these two fugitives get special investor status? What other high-level friendships had they cultivated in Moscow?

The local police and prosecutors won't want to entangle themselves in the pursuit of wealthy expat investors whose Russian papers are all in order.

As a career UN officer, Cheng naturally saw the matter quite differently.

These crimes were part of a direct attack on the cybersecurity of the UN and the SSP. They involved the destruction of life and property.

Bringing the criminals to justice would establish a precedent for future prosecutions and revitalize the UN Convention Against Organized Crime, which has been mostly dormant for three decades.

Cheng presented his analysis to Director Wang Shu, who immediately agreed about the importance of success in this investigation.

"You are quite right. This case is an opportunity for the UN to establish its right and ability to protect itself against cybercrime. Please proceed vigorously and use whatever resources are needed.

"I assume your next step is a trip to Moscow. I'll speak to the Secretary-General to request Russian cooperation through its UN Ambassador."

Director Wang had her own reasons for wanting the investigation to succeed. Capturing these blackmailers would generate positive media stories that show the UN as a competent and efficient institution. She also had personal motives—to protect Ibrahim and herself.

∞∞∞

Commander Fauré insisted that Kelly and Jay join Cheng on the trip to Moscow. Cheng worried about managing these amateurs, but he acceded to the Commander's wishes.

Anyway, Moscow is a big city, and tracking down the two suspects will probably require a lot of legwork. Kelly and Jay might help accelerate the search.

Ten days later, with Director Wang's enthusiastic support and the Russian UN Ambassador's assurance of assistance, the team departed for Moscow.

They arrived at the newly-rebuilt Sheremetyevo International Airport. A long taxi ride took them to the Metropol Hotel, a Moscow icon across from the Bolshoi Theater, adjacent to Revolutionary Square, and walking distance from the Kremlin.

After a fitful, jet-lagged night's sleep, Kelly joined Cheng and Jay for breakfast. Cheng had already called the UN Office in Moscow to let them know the group had arrived.

After breakfast, he met with the UN Office Deputy Secretary, Olaf Johansson. He asked for guidance on approaching the Moscow Police and notifying Russia's Federal Security Service and Foreign Intelligence Service of their presence. Johansson was forthcoming.

"As for notifying the Russian authorities, they already know of your arrival. Their immigration system tracks all diplomatic passport arrivals at Sheremetyevo, and they already contacted us to verify that you were legitimate UN representatives. Nothing further is necessary.

"The person to talk to in the Central Moscow Police Headquarters is Chief Officer Tschernovsky. I suggest you describe the purpose of your visit as a routine inquiry into some financial transactions with the SSPC that might have involved money laundering under the UN Convention Against Organized Crime.

"Ask him who to call if any difficulties arise. If possible, get a name and contact information. You don't want to wade through the police bureaucracy when you need urgent help.

"Tschernovsky might be willing to tell you what they know about your suspects. If they have not entirely gone underground, the Police should know who they are and what names they are using."

Johansson interrupted their conversation to call Tschernovsky. Speaking fluent Russian, he explained the circumstances of Cheng's visit to Moscow.

"I hope you can meet today with Cheng Yiming, a senior UN Investigator who leads the UN team. They have a lot to do in a brief visit."

"Of course, send them over. How about 1400?"

"Excellent. I'm sure 1400 will be convenient. He is hoping you can shortcut their search. The individuals they seek are expats with "investor status," so you probably have information about them."

"We'll see what we have when they get here."

"Thank you. I think I owe you a lunch. I'll send you a date soon."

Cheng, who knew enough Russian to grasp the essence of the conversation, thanked Johansson profusely. Johansson offered a few parting thoughts.

"Please keep us informed of your progress, especially if something goes wrong. I'll email you our emergency phone number and other contact information.

"On paper, you have the same diplomatic protection as foreign government officials on diplomatic passports. But getting that to work at the operational level may not be so smooth. We don't have the leverage of a national government to protect our personnel. So far, no UN employee has been held as a spy or criminal in Moscow, but you don't want to be the first.

"Thank you. We'll try not to cause you any trouble. Your contact information will be at hand, and we'll use it without hesitation if needed.

"I do have one other question. Is there any way for us to learn if our suspects passed any information to the Russian cybersecurity folks?"

"Not that I know of. We try to keep all of our own communications secret, but once your targets were here in Moscow, it wouldn't have been difficult for them to find customers for access to any UN computers."

Cheng left for his meeting with Tschernovsky, who offered no specific information about Jordan or Chris beyond their immigration status.

Aside from some routine bits of advice, he supplied Cheng with a letter of introduction verifying his credentials as a UN Inspector.

∞∞∞

Meanwhile, Kelly fidgeted in her room. Jay went to his room to review unrelated communications from the Commander. Being inactive while Cheng and Jay were working was annoying. Especially since she already knew what to do next.

I have the name of the bank and the recipient account where they wired the funds from Juba. I could go there right now and start tracing the funds. That's the most efficient way of finding Jordan and Chris.

By 1300, Kelly could sit still no longer. She texted Cheng and Jay.

"I'm going to the Moscow offices of the Bank of East Africa (BEA) to see what I can learn."

BEA, headquartered in Nairobi, was a recent arrival in Moscow. Kelly showed her SSPC ID and asked to speak with the Branch Manager. After a brief wait, the receptionist escorted her into Mr. Kamau Amora's office.

He listened to her explain that funds had been illegally wired from ICB Juba to a BEA account in this branch. Then he gave Kelly the usual excuse that bank records are confidential. Kelly pressed her argument.

"The global treaties on money laundering and transaction reporting require BEA to report all large transactions to the IMF. Failure to report could be a big problem for a small foreign bank in Moscow."

"I'm sure we would have reported transfers of that size, following BEA policy. It's also unlikely that a series of smaller transfers from the same bank in Juba slipped through the cracks.

"A small local branch can't always maintain the same level of oversight of its accounts as the large global banks here. But since you have the dates and the name of the originating bank, along with the account number here, it should be easy to find. I can certainly have it for you tomorrow."

Kelly smiled impatiently. "I would rather wait here until you find the information. Our team is only in Moscow for a few days, and we need to proceed as rapidly as possible. If you can just set me up with a computer and open the relevant files, I can search through them myself."

"I see. Well, if you don't mind conducting the search yourself."

Amora escorted her to an empty office and turned on the computer. He found the account and opened it for her. "Don't turn off the computer or look at any other account. The computer will immediately lock you out."

Two hours later, Kelly had reviewed the entire account. The records didn't seem complete, but Kelly went through them, making notes on the flows of funds.

She quickly concluded that Chris had disbursed all his incoming funds to other accounts and entities, mainly with Moscow business entity names.

One recipient, however, showed up frequently. It was a new account, created about two weeks after Chris's arrival in Moscow. A Nikolai Andreyevich owned the account and appeared to be using it for routine transactions. Andreyevich listed an address on Kuzitskiy Pereulok.

Kelly's intuition painted a picture. Her heart began beating faster.

Chris probably set up this account for himself in a Russian name to use for personal transactions.

Mr. Amora will probably call "Mr. Andreyevich" and alert him that someone from the UN is poking around in his account records. Maybe I can get to his address before he gets that message!

Kelly quickly packed up her notes. She was about to leave when she had another thought. Walking into Mr. Amora's office without knocking, she confronted him.

"I hope you haven't called Mr. Andreyevich about my presence here. Please do not do so. I didn't find any report to the IMF about the multiple incoming wired funds. I suggest you not say a word to anyone."

She did not stay to hear his answer. She wanted to catch up with Chris before he could get away. She hailed a taxi to Kuzitskiy Pereulok.

I must tell Jay and Cheng where I'm going now, just in case they are already wondering where I am—though they haven't bothered to call me so far. But I don't want to get an order to return to the Metropol immediately.

I'll just text them that I've found Chris's address and give it to them. If I don't see a reply, I can't do whatever it says!

Kelly turned off her phone.

Chapter 25

Pursuing Chris Kangata

CHENG STARED AT KELLY'S text. He was furious.

This kind of free-lancing is just what I feared. I can't afford to have this amateur disappear or die on my watch. I should have refused to take her along despite the Commander's insistence.

"Jay, do you know anything more than Kelly's text tells us?"

"No, sir. I didn't even know she left the hotel."

"Of course not. She knew you would stop her."

Cheng called Kelly; she didn't answer. He texted her. "Return to the Metropol immediately. You could be placing yourself at risk."

No answer to the text either.

"Damn it! I leave her alone for two hours, and she's off to the races. We don't know what she found or what she plans to do when she gets there. She didn't answer my call or text. She knows she should only turn off her phone if she's in trouble. But with her, it could just mean she doesn't want to hear from us."

Jay used Google Earth on his phone to look up the address Kelly had sent. Surveying the area, he noted the

Chekhovskaya Metro Station nearby. He showed the map to Cheng.

"Here's the address, close to the Chekhovskaya Metro Station. I imagine she took a taxi to the address she gave us. The Metro here is usually faster than a taxi. With any luck, we might even get there before she does."

Cheng whispered, "Let's go!" They hustled across Revolution Square to the Teatralnaya Metro Station. After 45 minutes of silent anxiety, they arrived at Chekhovskaya Station. Finding the precise address and building entrance would be more challenging, even with the online map's help.

∞∞∞

Kelly sat nervously in the taxi for over an hour, trapped in Moscow's notorious worst-in-the-world traffic. The location was relatively close-in, a prime address for anyone not living high on a corporate payroll.

The taxi dropped her on the street in front of the building. Baffled by the seemingly impregnable, doorless fortress, she eventually found a stranger who directed her to the back side's parking area.

She was surprised by the dilapidated-looking building entrance. Kelly congratulated herself on arriving. *At least I got here. I navigated this enormous city where I don't speak the language and found the place!*

Kelly poured over the listings on the video entry system and found Apt 604, the one on Chris's bank account. She triumphantly pushed the button. Someone let her in without a word. So someone was home, and she was inside the entrance door. But she had never thought beyond locating Chris. A chill ran down her spine as she recalled the old saying about the dog that caught the car.

Why would Chris let in a stranger? Is he expecting someone he doesn't know? Maybe he thought I was someone's friend who forgot the apartment number?

Or maybe Mr. Amora called him, and Chris has different plans for me. I'm dealing with a fugitive criminal, after all. Will I end up a hostage?

Suddenly Kelly realized how foolish she was to race to Chris's apartment.

I've no clue about what to do when Chris answers the door. I don't really even know if I will recognize him. I've only seen a few mug shots. Suppose it's someone else?

She stopped in the entrance area, frozen in fear of what might await her in 604. Her mind quickly cataloged the possible outcomes.

I could take out my gun and say I'm arresting him, which I'm not legally authorized to do. What if he just shoots me right then? A shoot-out would almost certainly mean my death, even if I do shoot him too. That's not what we came here to accomplish.

OK, so maybe he won't shoot, and I can hold him hostage while we wait for Cheng and Jay to show up—

but what if they aren't coming or don't get here for hours?

If I say my colleagues are on the way, that could give him even more reason to try to kill me and disappear. How long could I expect to hold him before he finds a way to turn the tables on me? He probably has a gun.

Maybe I could persuade him that being tried in New York for money-laundering and extortion would be a lot better than being convicted of murder in Moscow. Murder could mean the death penalty or life in Siberia if he got caught. IF HE GOT CAUGHT? Won't he assume he can escape?

I can't foresee any happy ending if I go to his door. Cheng and Jay must be furious with me for being so impetuous.

Another frightening vision crossed Kelly's scrambled brain. *Chris might come down here find me even if I don't go up. I'm at risk right here! My situation is impossible! I should have thought of all this before.*

Kelly prayed that Jay and Cheng would miraculously appear to save her and capture Chris. She suddenly remembered she had turned off her phone. Turning it on, she saw Jay and Cheng had each sent her multiple texts and phoned several times. The most recent one said they were coming to meet me here.

I'll be disgraced, punished for this thoughtless insubordination, and I deserve it. What will Jay think of me now?

∞∞∞

Jay was growing more anxious every minute. They finally arrived at the apartment's backside entrance just as Kelly was coming out. She tried to be casual and self-assured, but she couldn't carry it off.

Working to hold back her tears, she almost shouted, "Thank God you are here. Chris is in his apartment. He probably saw me on the entryway videoscreen when I buzzed. I couldn't figure out anything safe to do next."

Jay put his arm around Kelly and felt her body quivering. "You did the right thing to wait for us. But you should never have turned off your phone. You gave us a scare."

"I know. I'm sorry. I just turned it on. I see what a mistake it was."

Cheng just glared at Kelly in silence.

To change the subject, Kelly pointed to the buzzer labeled Apt 604. "He answered when I buzzed about 15 minutes ago. I haven't seen him come out."

"Is there a back entrance?"

Kelly hadn't thought to look. "I don't know. I didn't see any."

Cheng frowned and buzzed the apartment. Now there was no response. They buzzed other apartments until someone let them in. They climbed the stairs to 604 and knocked on the door, their guns drawn.

"Who is it?" someone asked.

"It's the police. Please open the door," Cheng replied softly. Chris opened the door, also with a gun in his hand.

"Don't do anything rash," Cheng whispered. "We're from the UN Security Management Service, and our objective is to return you to the United States for trial for extortion. We're only here to arrest you. We don't want any bloodshed."

Chris had no intention of surrendering. "You're in mortal danger right now, more I am. So put your guns down on the floor and step back away from the door."

Cheng and Jay complied.

"Now I'm going to walk out the door and disappear. Don't try to follow me; I know this neighborhood like the back of my hand, and I've prepared for this contingency."

He picked up a briefcase and walked out the door and down the stairs. As soon as Chris was out of sight, Jay reached for his gun. Cheng stopped him with a shake of his head.

"Following Chris could easily provoke a deadly gun battle in the stairway, or he might just be waiting outside for us to emerge. This is real life, not a movie where the good guys always win."

Cheng called Chief Tschernovsky to ask him to issue an all-points bulletin for Chris. He hoped they would catch him before he could leave the city.

Frustrated and still angry at Kelly, Cheng vented his justifiable fury.

"What did you expect to do here all by yourself? At least you were smart enough not to knock on his door alone. If he opened the door with a gun in his hand, what would you have done then?

"We might never have found you. Even if Chris didn't shoot you instantly, at some point he probably would have caught you off-guard and disarmed you. He'd have been smart to kill you and lock the apartment door as he left. No one would have found you for days."

Cheng paused.

"You're very fortunate to be alive. So now, let's get this straight. For as long as you are here with me, we're a team. You must never turn off your phone unless you are in mortal danger. Or go on solo adventures.

"Next time, I'll send you home for punishment for insubordination. SMS can't afford to lose UN personnel in a foreign capital like Moscow. And as it is, we've got to hope the Moscow Police catch Chris before he disappears.

Kelly sat down and bowed her head. "Yes, sir. I can see my actions were far more unsafe than I anticipated."

∞∞∞

Chris stopped running the moment he felt safe. He sent Jordan a text. Just two words: "Plan B."

Chapter 26

Airport Games

IT WAS ALREADY EVENING, BUT Cheng refused to rest. He took Jay to look for Jordan. He insisted that Kelly must stay at the hotel.

"You've done enough for one day. You need some rest to recover from the shock and excitement of your confrontation with Chris."

For once, Kelly was happy to obey.

Cheng was confident that Chris would alert Jordan one way or another. Jordan would not be as unprepared as Chris had been.

They began by investigating the addresses on the bank records. The first address was a rental apartment. "Charles Morgan" had moved out two weeks earlier. Cheng asked about a forwarding address and was rewarded with an address in the suburbs.

They immediately drove to the new location—a large western-style gated community of low-rise, multi-family apartment buildings. The guard on duty accepted Chief Tschernovsky's letter as sufficient evidence of Cheng and Jay's status.

Jay asked the guard if Jordan was at home. Receiving a positive response, he continued, "Is there any other exit from the community?"

"This is the only vehicle access, in or out."

"Thank you. Do not call Jordan." Cheng left for the residence alone.

Jay asked to see the gatehouse's computer records on Jordan and his vehicle. He sat down to read and print out the history of Jordan's visitors.

While Jay was busy, the guard surreptitiously signaled Jordan by buzzing him. Jordan knew the meaning of the gatehouse signal.

Making friends with the gatehouse guards always pays off! The police won't find me at home and unprepared.

Jordan already had a packed suitcase and a briefcase with his travel documents. Exiting through the rear door, he hustled to a small door in the community wall that runners used to reach a path through the woods.

The path intersected a primary boulevard in about two kilometers. Jordan called ahead for a driverless taxi to meet him there and take him to Sheremetyevo Airport.

∞∞∞

Cheng arrived at the apartment and asked the DoorGuard device for permission to enter. The machine answered, "No one is at home. I don't recognize your face. If you know the key code, say it now. Otherwise, please leave the premises."

"I was told by the gatehouse guard that Mr. Morgan is at home."

"No one is at home," the machine repeated.

"If you don't let me in, I will have to break down the door. I am authorized to do so by the Moscow Police Department. I can show you the letter." He held the letter up to the machine's eye.

"Thank you, but I have been instructed not to admit anyone when no one is home."

Cheng tried to see if he could learn anything more.

"When did the last occupant leave? Did you see where he went?"

"I'm not authorized to answer those questions."

Cheng gave up and drove back to the gatehouse, where he picked up Jay.

"He got away before I arrived. Is it possible the guard alerted him somehow?"

"I didn't hear him say anything to anyone. Maybe there was some other way.

"Did you find anything surprising?"

"Jordan has had visitors from the Syrian Embassy on a few occasions recently."

"Maybe he was already planning an escape route before we arrived in Moscow. Syria seems a likely destination, don't you think?"

He called Chief Tschernovsky. "Hello. Inspector Cheng here. We found our man's home, but he was expecting us. We think he's probably trying to get out of the country, likely heading for Syria, directly or indirectly.

"Can you put out a bulletin to hold up anyone traveling under the name of Jordan Milhaus or Charles Morgan?

"Yes, of course."

"Thank you. Excellent. We're on our way to Sheremetyevo right now. Who should we ask for when we arrive?"

"The Airport Police Chief is Gennady Kraznovich. A seasoned bureaucrat. Don't expect much."

"Thank you. I'll keep you posted."

Cheng explained Krasnovich's directions to Jay.

"When we arrive, I need to check in with Chief Gennady Kraznovich to find out whether he's searching for Jordan. You should go directly to the gate for the next flight to Damascus. If that's where Jordan is going, he's most likely to be at that gate."

Jay realized that instruction wouldn't work. "I think I need to go with you first. Without an official ID, I'll never get through security."

"Good point. But we need to be quick."

ооооо

Once in the taxi, Jordan made a reservation in the name of Charles Morgan. His flight would take him to Damascus, a rundown city still suffering from the aftermath of the decades-long civil war. The odds of anyone tracking him down there would be far lower than in Moscow.

Next, he called his friend Chief Gennady Kraznovich of the Sheremetyevo Airport Police Department.

"Gennady, Good morning. It's Charles Morgan. The gangsters are after me. They might try to stop me before I board my flight to Damascus. They claim they are UN officers, but that's their cover story. If they get their hands on me, I'll be dead in a day. Please ignore any request to detain me."

"I understand. What time is your flight? I won't have any way of disputing their paperwork if it comes from Central Moscow Police Headquarters. I can only delay following orders for a short time."

"My plane leaves in three hours. I'm on my way to Sheremetyevo right now. They won't know what flight I'm taking or where I'm going, so they will probably want you to insist on checking passenger lists on all flights. If you must search for me, I hope you can manage to leave the flights to Syria for last."

"I understand."

"Thank you. I won't forget your kindness."

"You've always been very generous."

∞∞∞

An hour later, Cheng and Jay had arrived at the terminal and found Chief Kraznovich's office. He welcomed them profusely and asked to see their credentials and the letter from Chief Tschernovsky, which he studied thoroughly. Finally, he asked how he could help.

"First, Jay needs credentials, so he can go through security and get to the gates for the flights to Damascus."

Cheng paused, waiting for a reply. Kraznovich said nothing. Cheng continued to wait. Kraznovich finally spoke.

"Is there anything else you want?"

"We both need airport security credentials, so we can get to the gates."

"Okay. I think I have what you need right here."

The Chief searched through his desk drawer, came up with nothing, and called his assistant. "Gregor, I don't seem to have any temporary security clearance badges in here. Can you bring me one—no, two?"

They sat in silence as they waited for Gregor.

After a few moments, Cheng continued.

"Second, it would be helpful to know what instructions you have issued to the airport staff. I assume you acted as Chief Tschernovsky requested."

"We can't upset the entire airport. Chief Tschernovsky told me where your suspect would be going, so I only alerted the desks covering Syrian flights. I told them to watch for a Charles Morgan, delay him, and call me. I haven't received any calls."

"What if he is flying under a different name? He's got a history of multiple names with passports to match. Did Tschernovsky mention the name Jordan Milhaus?"

"I don't recall any other name besides Morgan. Do you want me to add that name to the instructions?"

'Yes, please."

"Of course."

At that moment, Gregor entered the room and handed two badges to Kraznovich, who set them on his desk.

"Thank you, Gregor. You know that notice we sent out a few hours ago to the Syrian airline gates about Charles Morgan? It seems he might be flying under a different name—Jordan Millman, I think?"

He turned to Cheng. "Inspector Cheng, can you spell the man's name?"

Cheng fidgeted in his chair. "Of course. It's M-i-l-h-a-u-s. But can you please give Jay a badge, so he can get to the gate? Our suspect may not wait around long if the desk agent asks him to step out of line before boarding. Time is of the essence!"

"Certainly!"

He turned toward Jay. "I'll have it for you in a moment; I need to sign and date the badge and record the number. Protocols, you know. Can you spell your name for me?"

"S-a-n-j-a-y B-h-a-t-t-a-c-h-a-r." Kraznovich slowly and methodically wrote it on the badge and in his log.

"I assume you know how to get to the security checkpoints. I think you will want Concourse C, but check the signs for flights to Syria. This is a big airport. If you go through the wrong security gate, you may need to retrace your steps and go through security again."

Then he handed Jay the badge. Jay immediately rose, thanked the Chief, and rushed out the door.

Cheng, impatient with Kraznovich's slowness, struggled to restrain himself from shouting. He couldn't tell if Kraznovich was just naturally slow or was sandbagging their effort for some unknown reason.

"Can I please have my badge as well? And have you done anything to track our suspect if he decides to change his destination?"

"First things first." Chief Kraznovich picked up the other badge, asked for Cheng's full name, carefully signed and dated the badge, and entered it in his log. Then he answered the other question.

"Notifying every gate is impractical in this airport. We host 40 airlines, with daily flights to over 200 destinations. I suppose I can try if you like, but it's just a nuisance for the desk agents. The odds of catching him aren't good if he tries to take a flight at random."

"I understand, but please send the notice anyway."

"I'll have Gregor do it right away."

"Thank you, and thanks for all your help."

∞∞∞

Jay arrived at the gate for the SyrianAir flight to Damascus and approached the agent at the desk about the passenger list.

"Does the passenger list include 'Charles Morgan?'

The agent's eyes said no. "Is Jordan Milhaus on the passenger list?" That request drew a response that unavoidably telegraphed an affirmative answer.

"That would violate our instructions. We are not allowed to reveal any information about our passengers to strangers."

"I'm an official UN Investigator. That's why I have this badge. "Would you point him out to me, please?"

No response. Jay continued,

"You should have received a message from Police Chief Kraznovich telling you to detain anyone on your passenger list with the name either Charles Morgan or Jordan Milhaus. Did you receive that message?"

"Our instructions come from Syrian Arab Air Lines Corporation, not the local airport authorities. No, I did not see any such message, and I don't think we're authorized to follow such instructions if we receive them."

"But you work for the airport, not the airlines."

The gate agent paused.

"Well, yes, we do technically work for the Sheremetyevo Airport Authority, but our operating instructions on how to handle passengers come from the airlines."

Inspector Cheng arrived. He heard the last of the gate agent's responses to Jay.

"Sir," Cheng interrupted, "we don't care who you work for. We are trying to apprehend a dangerous criminal. If you do not identify this passenger to us, my only choice will be to announce that an armed criminal may be in the lounge.

"That certainly won't make either SyriaAir or the Airport authority happy. You might even lose your job for failing to assist officers of the law."

The gate agent said nothing and gave no indication he would change his mind.

Jordan was seated some distance from the desk. He could not hear all the conversation, but he quickly recognized that it turned into a controversy. Trying to look calm and nonchalant, he stood up and began walking out of the gate area.

Cheng had hoped that their target, eaves-dropping on the heated conversation, might try to disappear. When he spotted a man leaving the gate area, he pointed him out to Jay, who needed no instructions. Jay went after the man, still limping on his injured leg.

Cheng quickly surveyed the waiting passengers. He spotted Chris slouching in his seat with his back to the desk. Cheng quietly walked up behind Chris. Before Chris realized what was happening, Cheng grabbed his arm and handcuffed him to the row of chairs where he was sitting.

Turning to the agent, Cheng said in his fiercest tone, "Do Not Board Anyone On This Flight Until I Return!" Shocked by the drama, the agent nodded, and Cheng went after Jay.

ooooo

The airport was crowded, and Jay struggled to keep up with the man he assumed was Jordan. He had only a glimpse of his target. He was not optimistic he could identify the man again if he lost sight of him.

When Jay rounded the first turn in the concourse, the man had disappeared. He wasn't in line at any food concessions. Continuing to survey the area, he realized the man had probably ducked into the Men's Room.

∞∞∞

Cheng found Jay easily, just around the corner of the concourse. Jay explained the situation. "I believe he's in the Men's Room. Now you're here, I'll go in and get him."

"No, you won't. If he's in there, he's trapped. He has no place to go. And he still hopes eventually to get on a flight out of here. Patience is necessary, not action. Just stand by the bathroom door and ask for identification from every plausible man who emerges."

A few men came out right away. Jay stopped one of them, showed his badge, and asked for identification. Cheng leaned against the wall on the opposite side of the doorway. He could see each passenger's back as Jay questioned him. Soon the stream of exiting men dried up.

Jay was still impatient. Turning to Cheng, he said, "None of these men was the one. I should go in and see if anyone is left. If no one is there, we are letting him escape!"

"Absolutely not," Cheng replied. "If Jordan's not there, he's long gone. But if he is there, he is probably armed and positioned where he can shoot you on sight. He's already seen us, so he knows who we are. He's unlikely to take any chances. We just need to be more patient than he is. He's nervous. I doubt he'll last long."

Eight minutes later, one more man emerged from the Men's Room—with a pistol in his hand. He saw Jay and pointed the gun at him.

"I know who you are. I'm not about to turn myself in. So unless you want to die, just put your hands in the air, turn around slowly, and walk away."

Jay put his hands in the air and began to turn around.

At that instant, Cheng shouted, "Hey!" Simultaneously his hand came down forcefully on Jordan's arm, causing such pain that he dropped the gun. Before he could recover, Cheng locked Jordan's arm behind his back and put a handcuff on his wrist.

It was all over in a second. Jay was as surprised as Jordan and much more relieved.

"How did you do that?"

"Years of karate and jujitsu. While he was talking intensely to you, I quietly walked up behind him. When I shouted, he instinctively turned to see who was behind him.

"The risk was whether he could fire at you before I could disarm him. I waited until he finished talking and was satisfied you were cooperating. At that point, his grip would have relaxed, and a shot would have gone wild. He only had a fraction of a second before I hit his arm.

"I don't think I broke his arm, but it's hard to calibrate a maneuver like that. I'll take him to the airport medical center to check for injuries. But first, please go back to the gate and let the agent board the other passengers to Syria. Call the Airport Police to take Chris into custody. I handcuffed him in the waiting area before I came to find you.

"Then call Director Wang, report our success in capturing Jordan and Chris, and ask her to get Chief Tschernovsky to cooperate with an informal rendition of Chris and Jordan to the US. That will require two armed SMS agents or New York Police to handle returning the suspects to New York."

"Yes, sir."

Jay called Wang and transmitted Cheng's message, along with a blow-by-blow account of the captures. Wang was delighted.

"That's the best news today! I guess we don't need to worry about paying the blackmail money. You sound more excited than frightened. Have you enjoyed working with Cheng?"

"He's amazing! I'm sure I could learn a lot from him, from strategies to tricks of the trade. I suppose he's done this all his life, so today was just another day for him. But if he hadn't stopped me from following my amateur instincts, I'd probably be dead, and one of our suspects would have escaped."

"He's my best investigator – fearless and thoughtful in the right combinations. I'm glad you enjoyed the experience. Let me know if you want to do more."

"Thank you. I'll think about it."

Jay's next call was to Commander Fauré.

"I'm pleased to report that we caught both of our suspects, and Director Wang will be arranging for their return to New York for prosecution."

"Excellent. I'll be eager to hear the whole story when you return. Have you learned anything about their computers and documents? It would be good to know if they shared their knowledge with anyone.

"Jerry Stephens has plugged the keyhole that CDI discovered, but once someone with resources realizes the value of being able to move mirrors, they will be looking for new ways to take control of them.

"I haven't thought about that, sir. Our prisoners both had carry-on bags that might have the most valuable material. Their residences probably contain more documents that will be useful for prosecuting them and identifying anyone they may have offered their knowledge.

"I'll talk to Director Wang about how SMS can get access to their baggage and homes. I don't know what level of cooperation the UN gets from the Russian police. They seem to have been helpful so far."

"If she wants you to stay there to follow up, I'm happy to have you stay in Moscow to finish up the operation."

"Thank you, sir. I'll let Director Wang know."

Chapter 27

Free Time in Moscow

THE AIRPORT DOCTOR CONCLUDED that Jordan was not seriously injured. She gave him two aspirin.

Cheng and Jay transported Jordan to the Airport Police jail, where Chris was already in custody. Cheng called Tschernovsky to send Moscow Police to arrest Jordan and Chris formally and hold them for extradition.

Kelly was waiting impatiently at the Metropol for their return. Fearful for Jay's safety, she was incapable of doing anything constructive.

When they finally arrived, she insisted on a step-by-step reprise, ostensibly to serve as the basis of their formal report to Director Wang and Commander Fauré, but really to banish her anxiety.

Jay insisted he was never in as much danger as she had been. Cheng assured her that they always had complete control of the situation. "I've been training for occasions like this for 20 years and used karate three times before. The idea is to surprise and disarm the suspect without unnecessary force or injury," Cheng explained.

ꝏꝏꝏ

Calmer now, Kelly changed the topic. "So, what is the plan now?"

Cheng responded immediately. "It's Friday night. I hope to take the late flight home. I've seen Moscow before. You need to stay here until the escort guards arrive.

"I'm sure the Commander would not object to you staying for the weekend or even taking a few days of leave. It's the only reward international service can offer for all you've done here—both of you.

"There's a lot to see and do in Moscow—great art museums; outstanding restaurants with cuisine from all over the world; spectacular classical music, ballet, and opera; and shops selling whatever you want."

Kelly smiled. "Thank you. That sounds delightful—I've never been anywhere near here before. I'll certainly take advantage of the opportunity."

She looked over at Jay, who avoided her eyes as he responded. "Director Wang has asked me to stay in Moscow to coordinate with the New York and Moscow police on delivering the prisoners. Then I hope I can get authorization to search their residences for evidence. So I'll remain for at least a few days next week."

Kelly did her best to hide her rejoicing about a weekend in Moscow with Jay. Whatever Cheng might surmise, making her enthusiasm evident could display an unprofessional interest in Jay's company. She said nothing.

Anyway, it's all arranged. One wrong word from me could just remind Jay of his anxieties about me. From my perspective, it's a unique opportunity. But I don't want him to feel pushed. He needs to sort it out for himself.

Jay turned to Cheng. "Do you want us to see you off? We owe you a great deal, including saving both of our lives."

"Thanks, that won't be necessary. Honestly, I'll enjoy some time to myself to rest and decompress from the excitement of the day. I'll see you in New York." With that, Cheng left for his room.

Jay smiled enigmatically at Kelly. "I suggest we get room service for dinner and turn in early tonight. Tomorrow we can visit some museums. I'll make a dinner reservation at Café Pushkin, supposedly one of the best in the city. Does that sound okay?"

"Perfect. I'm glad you are staying. I wasn't looking forward to navigating Moscow alone. We can choose our first tourist destinations at breakfast and more at dinner."

Kelly slept soundly. In the morning, she dressed in comfortable tourist clothes. After breakfast, they wandered through the Moscow Museum of Modern Art, which features 20th Century Russian artists. Many of the works in its collection had never been exhibited in the West. Their conversations were cheerful and intellectual, mostly about how Russian art reflects Russian history and culture.

They returned to the hotel in time for naps before dinner. Kelly felt she was walking on eggshells, unable to resolve her torment over the situational ambiguity. She carefully considered how to dress and behave for the evening.

I want to look attractive but not alluring. I have no idea what Jay is thinking about tonight. He might think it's an opportunity to enjoy our relationship once again.

Or he might be determined to maintain an entirely professional relationship. If I'm the slightest bit aggressive, I could ruin it all.

She put on the only social dress she had packed—a simple black dress with pearl earrings and a scarf.

I know what I want, but I'm not going to undermine my professional reputation or friendship with Jay for a few nights of sex in Moscow. Even with Jay.

She left for the ornate Metropol lobby to meet Jay, trying to keep those thoughts in mind.

Jay was also nervous about the evening and the rest of the weekend. *I know what I should do, but can I hold out for two more nights? And who would benefit if I did or didn't? I've already crossed the line twice. I already told her "never again" after the first time, but then surrendered in Wuhan.*

I wonder what she expects. Maybe she's moved on. I don't want to initiate anything that becomes awkward for her. We are having an enjoyable and enriching weekend without physical contact so far.

Kelly and Jay walked out into a beautifully chilly, sunny late March evening and took the Metro to the Chekhovskaya Station. The Café Pushkin was only a short walk on Tverskoy Boulevard from Pushkin Square. Pushkin had lived in this neighborhood for many years.

The Café was a unique Moscow landmark. Its creation was inspired by a wildly popular French song, "Natalie," in which the singer fantasizes about his young Russian tour guide:

> We are walking around Moscow, visiting Red Square, and you are telling me learned things about Lenin and the Revolution. But I'm thinking,
>
> 'I wish we were at Café Pushkin, looking at the snow outside the windows. We'd drink hot chocolate, and talk about something completely different...'

No such Café existed at the time of the song or for the next 30 years, though French tourists in Moscow frequently asked for it. The real Café Pushkin opened in the last years of the 20th Century.

The building housing the Café was designed in the 1780s by Italian architects as a home for a retired Russian nobleman who had served as Catherine the Great's Ambassador to Italy. About forty years later, a subsequent owner of necessity converted it into an elegant pharmacy and tearoom, with an extensive library and a collection of antique scientific instruments.

The original appearance had been preserved, including the. The menu was a combination of authentic Russian and elegant French cuisine.

Kelly and Jay were seated in the "library," with dark wood paneling and elaborate chandeliers. They were happy with the quiet table for two set against a wall of books.

Their conversation was somewhat stilted at first, recounting their investigative successes and respective moments of terror. After the first glass of champagne, the conversation grew livelier. They assembled the rest of their weekend: The State Museum of Oriental Art, Red Square and St. Basil's Cathedral, and the museums inside the Kremlin.

They reserved tickets for appealing performances at the Bolshoi Theater and the Moscow Conservatory of Music. By the time the main course arrived, they had planned a whirlwind tour more suitable for a week than a weekend.

Then they just enjoyed each other's company as if they had been friends for years. Jay talked freely about his son. Kelly spoke enthusiastically about her first opportunity for free time in a foreign capital with a rich cultural history.

When they returned to the Metropol, the earlier awkwardness reappeared. Neither knew how to end the evening without making a gesture that might spoil the weekend. Finally, Kelly just opened her heart.

"Jay, I want the closest possible relationship with you—physical, mental, emotional. I hope you know I will never do anything to hurt you personally or professionally.

"I'm fully aware of the potential risks for both of us, from each other and the world around us. If your 'never again' applies in Moscow, I will still treasure our time here and work harmoniously with you back home.

"The decision about these nights is entirely yours. Whatever you decide, I want you to know I'm in love with you, and I'm sure I will love you for the rest of my life."

Jay stared at Kelly with tears in his eyes. After a momentary pause, he took her in his arms, kissed her, and led her gently to his room.

The rest of their time together was like a fairytale honeymoon. Moscow's museums, historic sites, and brilliant music and dance were dazzling. They dined and laughed and held hands and made love. Jay accompanied Kelly to the airport Tuesday morning. They said goodbye without angst or regrets, intoxicated by their once-in-a-lifetime experience in Moscow.

Kelly was alone on the plane and then alone in her apartment, but she kept reliving her moments with Jay. She wanted to share her feelings with Maureen, but feared once she said the words aloud, they would seep into conversations with others. She vowed not to tell anyone about their Moscow vacation or her love for Jay. It was personal history, just for her.

∞∞∞

At the end of his next regular weekly meeting Commander Fauré, Jay asked for a few extra moments.

"Sir, I'd like to discuss a change in my career path. My brief foray into the world of law enforcement was far more satisfying than I expected.

"Working for you is a pleasure; you are the best superior I could imagine. I've learned a lot from you about management that I'm sure will prepare me well for my future.

"But at this point, worrying about budgets, organizational reports, and personnel matters does not compare to the drama of security and law enforcement. I'm eager to try it, at least for a while. I want to learn more from Cheng, face new challenges to my wits and skills every day, and travel the world.

"Director Wang casually mentioned the idea to me, and I hope you will speak with her about transferring me to a position where I can learn the craft and take on greater responsibilities."

Commander Fauré, surprised, sat back in his chair.

"I can understand your desire to pursue a career that'll bring excitement and challenge to your life. That's why I entered military service myself. I also see my position here as a path to an even more exciting role.

"You've performed outstandingly. I'll recommend you in the strongest terms to Director Wang. I expect she will accept my advice and take you on in a position with career potential, and I'm confident you will do well there."

"Thank you, sir, for those kind words and your willingness to help. I'll do everything I can to ensure you never regret recommending me.

"I have thought about what you need here to replace me. I have observed Officer O'Rourke at close range in stressful circumstances over the last month while working with me in Wuhan and Inspector Cheng and me in Moscow.

"She's ambitious, intelligent, capable, and creative. She has matured since her younger days. She's eager to show what she can do.

"I think she'd be an outstanding Executive Assistant for you. Of course, she'll need guidance at first, but I believe you'll be pleased with her performance."

Commander Fauré was quite surprised by Jay's recommendation. It reinforced his suspicions that Jay and Kelly were more than just friends.

Perhaps Jay's transfer is a wise idea for other reasons as well. As for Kelly, the adage is, "hold your friends close, and your enemies closer." Working for me will keep Kelly busy with productive tasks, and her obsession with the mirror realignments will fade.

"I appreciate hearing your judgment. It would be a jump for her. She only recently passed her exams. She was first in her class, but other more senior officers will also want your position, and fairness demands careful evaluation of all applicants.

"But I've often seen that a new person with the right talent is a better choice than a journeyman who has put in his time but lacks the creative energy and talent I need."

"Thank you, sir. I understand that the decision is a complex one. Perhaps you might give Officer O'Rourke an interim appointment while you conduct a formal search. That way, you can see how she handles her responsibilities. It would be good for her to have been your Executive Assistant even for a short time."

"That might work. Let me talk to HR."

∞∞∞

Kelly didn't know what to think when Jay invited her to dinner a week later.

I can't think of any professional reason for it. I suppose he wants me to know that our weekend must be the end.

She was bewildered when he announced that he would be leaving his position with the Commander and the SSPC. All she could hear was that he would be gone. Her feelings were profoundly negative.

"Why would you want to do that? Isn't this a step down? You won't be working for the Commander anymore! You won't be around here anymore!"

Catching her breath, she realized he had already made his decision. She changed her tone.

"I guess I shouldn't be so astonished. I could see how much you enjoyed our work in Wuhan and Moscow. And Cheng could teach you a lot. I'm sure you will do very well in that world. But I'm terrified by the thought you will be in constant danger. You were already wounded once, and you survived two close encounters in Moscow.

"I can't tell you how secure I have felt since our first drinks together, just knowing you were here in the SSPC, despite our infrequent contact. I'll feel uneasy not knowing where you are or what you are doing, especially given the risks.

"I see it's what you want, and I know you are well suited to it. But I'll miss your presence here every day."

Kelly paused for a moment, hoping those words would carry as much meaning to Jay as they did to her.

When Jay told her about his recommendation that she replace him, she was overwhelmed.

"I'm honored that you would even suggest me as your successor. It'd be quite a promotion to serve there, even as an interim appointee. I hope I will be up to the task. I'll do my best not to embarrass you if it happens. Thank you."

Jay saw the intensity of Kelly's emotions, but he wanted to avoid revealing his own feelings. He quickly redirected the conversation to inconsequential matters and eventually said goodnight without comment on the future.

Kelly couldn't help but speculate about what Jay's decision told her about his feelings toward her.

I wonder how much the desire to end our unprofessional relationship drove his decision. I wish I could discuss it with him, but I'm not strong enough for that without breaking down in tears.

His transfer could make it easier for us to be together, but it's more likely he will soon forget me. There are plenty of other fish in the sea for him.

∞∞∞

Thirty days later, Jay reported to Director Wang as her Special Assistant and began training in security techniques and skills. Inspector Cheng gave him regular coaching and valuable insights. He was enjoying every minute of his new position.

Commander Fauré selected Kelly as his interim Executive Assistant. She was on cloud nine. She called Maureen to share her excitement.

"Hi, sis. I told you that I had the best grade on the Induction Exam among all the recruits. Thanks to Jay, the Commander selected me to replace Jay as his Executive Assistant. It's only an interim appointment because the position description calls for a more experienced officer. But I hope once he sees how dedicated I am, maybe he'll keep me."

Maureen was pleased, but other thoughts come to her mind for Kelly.

"From what you've told me about the Commander, he would be quite a catch. Do you think your attractiveness had anything to do with his decision?"

Kelly bristled at the thought. She recognized that the Commander would be a desirable mate, but he was not the one she wanted.

"I certainly hope not! And if that's what he has in mind, he'll be sorely disappointed. I'm not interested in another office romance."

"Well, don't run away if he expresses a personal interest in an appropriate way. You don't want to spend your life alone."

"Thanks, sis, but I still want Jay. The right man is worth waiting for."

"Of course, my dear." Maureen knew better than to pursue the subject. Kelly would just dig in deeper.

Kelly also questioned whether expecting Jay to return was a fantasy, but she would never say so to Maureen.

Kelly over the next few months, Kelly found an occasional excuse to call Jay for background on a project she had inherited from him. The conversations were always professional, even when she asked about his son.

Slowly she became reconciled to the idea their personal lives would never intersect again. She suppressed every urge to express her continuing desire to be with him.

∞∞∞

Kelly rapidly learned everything there was to know about the SSPC mission, the mirror shield technology, and the complex bureaucratic processes necessary to make the SSPC run smoothly and efficiently.

She sometimes struggled to catch up with the Commander's wide-ranging and impossibly urgent demands. But the fact that Jay and the Commander had expressed confidence in her helped get through the difficult early days. And she loved the challenges awaiting her each day.

Commander Fauré was quickly impressed by Kelly's talent and dedication. Their relationship was thoroughly professional from the first day. The Commander was too disciplined and too busy to allow Kelly's style and character to distract him.

Kelly grew better at the job with every passing month. After six months, Fauré told his HR Director to take the necessary steps to make her eligible for selection for the permanent position. When the time came, he selected her as his permanent Executive Assistant.

Too excited and still too emotional to handle a videocall with Jay, she sent him a text message.

"Commander Fauré informed me today that he has selected me as his permanent Executive Assistant. This appointment means the world to me. Thank you again for everything."

Jay responded in equally spare terms. "I'm delighted at the news of your selection. It's what I thought would happen. I know you deserve it. Congratulations and best of luck."

Kelly never gave up hoping that Jay would return one day. In the meantime, her work was her only love.

Part VI

Chapter 28

Fauré Confronts His Dilemmas

THE CAPTURE OF CHRIS AND Jordan put an end to the insurance racket and the blackmail scheme. But the problem of the shadows over tropical tourist resorts remained. Commander Fauré had frozen Mirrors 170, 210, 220, and 226 in their current positions, pending final decisions about their realignment.

He needed to encourage Mohamed Ibrahim to live without immediate, specific relief.

"MSTY, please invite Director Mohamed Ibrahim for a lunch meeting at The LCL Bar and Kitchen in the Westin Grand Central. The quietest table they have."

"Yes, Sir."

Commander Fauré arrived early for lunch so as not to keep Ibrahim waiting. To his surprise, Ibrahim was already at the table. After the usual pleasantries, they ordered lunch. Fauré came to the point.

"I have thought long and hard about our earlier conversations and the situation facing the tourist facilities in the Maldives and other tropical locations.

"Since we last talked, I have personally reviewed the comments in response to the Notice proposing to realign mirrors for the benefit of tropical tourist locations. As I anticipated, similar facilities in three other Asian countries expressed equally severe financial viability concerns. They strongly object to piecemeal adjustments to the SSP Master Plan that could give their competitors an advantage.

"I have also learned that the tourism industry's concerns pale in comparison to real and imagined threats to subsistence farming and fishing communities about moving shadows to or from the places of their livelihoods.

"The SSPC established the original mirror locations using the best scientific and technological information available. The SSPC inherently creates losers as well as winners. The fundamental goal is to minimize losses and maximize global gains.

Making adjustments in response to political or industrial sector pressures, rather than the best science, would undermine the presumption of integrity on which the entire UN SSP depends. I know that you, as an astute participant in the SSP's creation, understand that the survival of the SSP depends on public confidence in its integrity.

"We will initiate a systematic program review this year to consider everything we now know about the SSP's impacts, positive and negative, on all economic sectors. That analysis will include everything we've learned about the tropical tourism industry.

"In the meantime, I can't take an action that will benefit only the Maldivian tourist resorts. I can't even promise the original mirror alignments will ever change.

"I've also heard concerns about the appearance created by the Notice, that a Governing Board Member's particular interests might be getting special consideration.

"I am not at all suggesting that your actions are anything other than an honest, unbiased desire to see the SSP serve everyone's best interests, and I will say so.

"But based on all these factors, I intend to replace the proposal with a new Notice also asking for comments on urgent needs beyond tropical tourist resorts.

"I wanted to let you know in person. I apologize for my mistake in thinking I could fix this problem informally, and I hope I have not done any serious damage."

Director Ibrahim sat silently for a few moments, working to collect his thoughts and subdue his feelings about the supposed disclaimer of any misconduct on his part and Fauré's failure to mention that he implicitly sought a favor in return.

"I understand your position. It is unfortunate you did not foresee these ramifications when we first talked. You had already told me that procedural requirements would delay the process. Now you are telling me that ever providing relief to the Maldives tourist resorts, or tourist resorts in general, is uncertain.

"You are disregarding the immediate and potentially drastic financial impact of the SSPC's abstractly designed program on an industry that is vital to the economic health of several Asian island economies.

"And I fear you are underestimating the tropical tourism industry's expectations and the political impact of the industry's hostility to the SSP program. I hope you will rethink your decision and consider ameliorating the damage to all affected tourist communities.

"Thank you for giving me this advance notice. I do appreciate it. I look forward to hearing the final results of your further consideration of the matter."

With that, Mohamed rose and departed. Fauré was left to consider his doubts, which were acute.

Maybe I'm not making the right decision after all? I made a mistake by starting down this road in secret, but does that mean that making fractional mirror realignments to avoid critical damage to the Asian tourist industry is wrong?

My decision shouldn't be driven by self-righteous moralism, an obsession with preserving my reputation, or the sensibilities of some young Chinese computer engineers who have no real decision-making experience.

I suppose I could recuse myself and allow someone else to decide. But who—The Board? The Science Advisory Committee? That would protect me.

Commander Fauré sat back in his chair, weighing this option in his mind. His conclusions emerged slowly.

No. I should consult the Board and the Committee, but I am the Commander, and I bear the final responsibility. Making decisions on matters with multiple global and local impacts is inevitably messy. My charge is to achieve results that serve humanity with minimal damage to particular communities.

∞∞∞

Mohamed decided to stay in New York another evening. He needed to talk things through with Wang Shu, the most astute strategist he knew. After dinner, he outlined Commander Fauré's statements at lunch and expressed his anger and disappointment with the decision.

"I haven't been paid by anyone to lobby SSPC to change its plan. The Maldivian tourist operators weren't expecting others to ask for similar treatment. However, the operators of comparable facilities elsewhere in Asia will insist that the SSPC treat their areas similarly.

Fauré tells me there would be no adverse effect from realigning a few mirrors. So no one would be harmed by the decision.

"Naturally, I expected the Maldives operators to appreciate my efforts if I succeeded. They would undoubtedly remember my help if I'm ever a candidate for Foreign Minister or Prime Minister. That's the way the political world works.

"I also expected Fauré to appreciate my work for him on the Malkovich expense probe. I kept him from the danger of embarrassment, and he knows it.

"I suppose he's right that there is an apparent conflict of interest that could hurt both of us. Maybe I should suggest that the Commander defer to the Board on this decision and get us both out of the line of fire. What do you think?"

Wang felt barred from telling Mohamed about NSSI hacking MSTY and illegally offering to make changes to the mirror shadows.

It's up to the Commander to decide whether and when to tell his Board. I can't share this story with anyone. But I'm afraid Mohamed's request and Fauré's initial realignment of Mirror 170 might surface if Jordan or Chris goes to trial. That revelation could end the Commander's and Mohamed's public careers. They could never put to rest the charges of conflict of interest and self-aggrandizement.

I don't know what to advise him about dealing with the Commander. The risks of tainted reputations remain no matter what they do.

Instead, she raised a more radical possibility, one that had been on her mind for some time.

"Mohamed, my love, maybe it's time for us to exit the tangled jungle of public service. Why don't we just both take invisible jobs in New York or Washington? Haven't you had enough of shuttling back and forth?

"Becoming Foreign Minister or Prime Minister would mean years living in Malé, constant airplane travel, and nights alone in hotel rooms at cookie-cutter hotels around the world. Would Adeela be happy in Malé, spending most of her time alone?

"So what would Adeela say about moving to New York? She must know you see someone here. She's never confronted you. What would happen if you stopped pretending?

"She grew up in a world where men have multiple wives. You've always been a good husband and father. She knows you care for each other. She needs to know you will never divorce her. Maybe that's all she needs.

"As for me, I love you, but I've never expected an exclusive relationship. My work doesn't allow time for it anyway. I'm comfortable continuing our lives with that understanding, either here or in Washington.

"We've been at this public policy business all our lives. We've accomplished a great deal. Suppose we take a different, less stressful path?"

Mohamed had long envied the more pleasant and sane life of colleagues in the private sector. But he was stunned by Wang's words.

"I always assumed that you would never give up your public ambitions, and you expected the same from me. Your suggestion opens a world of new possibilities. Maybe you're right.

"But would you give up the UN? Could you live in the same city as Adeela? Suppose she insists we stay in Washington, where she has friends?"

Wang had already thought about these questions.

"Honestly, I'm not making policy at the UN, the way we did a decade ago advocating the creation of the

Solar Shield. My security work is essential, but it doesn't change the world.

"I would be happy living in the same city as Adeela if it meant I would see you a little more often and with less discomfort for you. I wouldn't be the first career woman in Washington with a married lover. And Adeela definitely wouldn't be the first Washington wife whose husband has a mistress.

"I'm sure I could find a satisfactory job to keep me feeling useful, without the high profile. So think it over. We can talk more later.

∞∞∞

Five weeks later, after consulting with SSPC's Science Advisory Committee and the Board of Directors and weighing the options, Commander Fauré announced his decision.

He did not withdraw the Notice, and he did not initiate the lengthy and uncertain comprehensive review he had described to Ibrahim.

Instead, he approved immediate adjustments to the perpendicular deviation of six SSP mirrors, including 170, 210, 220, and 226. He justified his decisions based on public comments that they were necessary to avoid drastic and unforeseen financial impacts on tropical resort facilities. They were all relying on realignments that would preserve sunlight for their guests.

He postponed action on the many other realignments that various industries advocated in their comments. He promised a more comprehensive consideration of additional changes after the Shadows Impact Study provided the necessary guidance.

The following paragraphs in the SSPC Decision Document explain his conclusions:

> The SSPC Commander is taking this decision after consultation with the Board of Directors and the SSPC Science Advisory Committee.
>
> Many public comments assert the existence of adverse economic effects on other industries and communities besides tourism. They claim that their circumstances deserve similar adjustments.
>
> Unfortunately, the SSPC does not currently have the necessary data or technical capability to evaluate realignments that arguably benefit other industries. We cannot say with sufficient confidence that they will not have adverse effects that would outweigh the claimed benefits.
>
> SSPC is accelerating the Shadows Impact Study, which will examine data from on-the-ground observations of shadow impacts rather than the modeled impacts that the SSPC necessarily used to determine the current mirror placements.
>
> The results of the Shadows Impact Study will lead to a new Proposal for further revisions to the SSP Master Plan. The Proposal will analyze the current mirror shadows and the costs and benefits of proposed changes.
>
> SSPC reserves the authority to initiate further mirror alignments after Public Notice, even before completing the full Shadows Impact Study if available data clearly demonstrates that current

shadows are imposing adverse effects that a realignment can reduce without noticeably affecting the overall efficacy of the SSP.

Like all decisions about mirror locations, today's decision inevitably involves a degree of subjectivity and discretion. The SSPC hopes today's actions will continue to justify the confidence the UN and Earth's people have placed in our hands.

Chapter 29

Celebrations In 2037

APRIL 22, 2037, WOULD MARK the Fifth Anniversary of the launch of the last six of the 480 mirrors comprising the Solar Shield. At Commander Fauré's direction, Kelly began arranging an anniversary celebration at the Houston Space Center.

Her tasks included everything associated with the event: assembling the guest list, sending invitations and tracking responses, and planning the day's programs, from welcome ceremonies to panel discussions to dinner speakers.

Kelly arranged for the reception area to include continuous loop videos of past launches. Panel discussions about climate change described and evaluated the Solar Shield's effectiveness in slowing the rate of global warming.

The slower pace of global warming was allowing human civilization and all life on the planet more time to adapt to the ongoing climate changes. For the most short-lived species, the process of evolution could now keep pace with the rate of climate changes. The slowdown was averting many hundreds of plant, animal, and insect extinctions.

For human society, the slower pace of change meant more time to reinforce infrastructure, relocate victim populations, and transform techniques for producing energy, food, and the multitude of goods and services used in contemporary life.

∞∞∞

Kelly carefully tracked all the acceptances, especially awaiting Jay's response. When it finally arrived, she anxiously opened the e-envelope.

Yes, he is coming, and he's coming alone!

Though still responsible for the event's hundreds of little details, her mind now wandered to thoughts of Jay.

That could mean anything, of course. Maybe he has a wife or lover who would feel out of place here, not knowing anyone. Maybe he's coming to talk to someone about a new job. Probably he'll just come for the day, say hello, and be gone.

But I hope he still wants to see me again after Wuhan and Moscow. Dare I imagine they still mean as much to him as they do to me?

I'll need to be careful how I behave around him in public. I'll be too busy to spend any time with him during the day anyway. But I don't want him to think I'm avoiding him.

Should I contact him before he comes? What would I say? Should I let him know I won't have any time during the day? No. That would be presumptuous. Our relationship, if any, still rests in his hands.

When Jay arrived at the registration desk, Kelly was busily supervising the process, giving instructions to the staff and helping guests who needed advice. When she turned in his direction, he smiled with an unmistakable warmth. Kelly was overwhelmed at seeing him but did her best to hide her emotions.

Jay was equally pleased but cautious.

I hope she wants to see me. I've never forgotten her, and I want her in my life now more than ever. Maybe she's found someone new. Perhaps the Commander? That would be scandalous, but Kelly is irresistible. If she broke the rules with me, she might do the same with him. The Commander is precisely the man she should want. I don't want to embarrass myself, but there's only one way to find out, and that's to ask.

He had painstakingly prepared his first words.

"Hello! It's nice to see you again. I'm sure you're busy during the day today, but I hope you can spend a little time with me this evening or tomorrow at breakfast."

Seeing Kelly's enthusiastic smile, he continued, "I'm staying at the Marriott across the street—room 1156. Leave a message there if you have some time."

Kelly waited until later in the day to leave a message. "I'll try to come by this evening, but it will be late. I can't leave here until after the last guest. I will be free for breakfast."

Kelly happily drowned herself in the minutia of assuring that each event and activity proceed as intended. The highlight of the dinner was a short speech by former US President Biden. He had prodded the US Congress and the UN General Assembly and Security Council to endorse the Solar Shield in 2025 during his second term.

Commander Fauré was delighted with the impressive panel discussions and the flawless execution of each event. He made a note to reward Kelly with a bonus and a small promotion.

Kelly eventually made her way to Jay's hotel. They were both tired from a long day. At first, the conversation was mundane, but it warmed as they reminisced about their travels together.

"I confess I had reservations about taking you to Moscow. I was afraid it would be unsafe, and I was right."

Kelly reassured him. "I knew going to Moscow could involve dangers, but I was crazed whenever you were out of sight, not knowing what was happening to you."

Memories of the weekend in Moscow suddenly engulfed her. She couldn't stop the words she wanted to say from gushing out.

"Jay, I wouldn't have passed up our weekend in Moscow for anything. It was the most important and wonderful experience in my life."

She wanted to say, "I still miss you every day," but she feared she had already said too much.

Jay took her hand. "I have important news. After two more wounds and some other close calls, I'm leaving investigative work at SMS. You may know

Director Wang resigned from SMS, and Cheng is her successor. He's asked me to be his Deputy.

"It's a significant promotion. More important, I'll be back at UN Headquarters and no longer putting my life in danger. More important, I didn't pursue you while my life was constantly at risk. I knew you would be tormented whenever I went on a mission.

He suddenly paused. "But now everything will be different. I could offer you a stable life and a secure home.

"I hope tonight isn't just a one-night hello for you."

Kelly began to cry. Wiping her eyes, she replied, "Of course not. I've dreamed of spending my life with you since our first dinners together. If this is a proposal, I accept with enthusiasm!"

"I hadn't planned it this way, but yes, that is what I mean."

Kelly kissed him intensely. All conversation ended. The night and morning were lost in ecstasy as they dared to believe their dreams were coming true. At breakfast, they began planning their future together.

Making life fit together for two career professionals in the UN raised the potential for complications. But they were determined to make it work one way or another. Envisioning a home together in New York was a joyful exercise.

∞∞∞

Wang Shu and Mohamed Ibrahim also attended the fifth-anniversary celebration. Ibrahim had left the

World Bank and the SSPC Board. Now he was managing the Asian Green Infrastructure Program of a major private international investment bank.

Wang Shu relocated to Washington to coordinate security services for the International Monetary Fund. Technically it was a step down from overseeing security for the entire United Nations system, But the pay and benefits were equivalent, and the demands were much less intense.

Ibrahim was more relaxed about their relationship now that he had discussed it with Adeela. She accepted the circumstances as fate, having concluded long ago concluded that Ibrahim must have a New York lover. Ibrahim reassured her that Wang didn't threaten their future. Washington would be their home indefinitely.

The Fifth Anniversary materials revealed that Ambassador Mohamed Ibrahim, Wang Shu, and two other diplomats had masterminded the original "tropospheric veil" project. This public revelation captured media attention around the world.

Ibrahim and Wang were hailed as heroes after all the years of secrecy. For Wang, the recognition was a reminder of the heady days when the world of diplomacy and politics opened unlimited possibilities for a future of power and fame. She had chosen to pursue her love instead, and she had no regrets about her choice.

THE END

GLOSSARY OF ACRONYMS

CDI — Computer Defense, Incorporated, a private cybersecurity firm founded by Zhang Xingwen and Cai Jin

IMF — International Monetary Fund, a UN-related international financial organization

₣ — IMF Electronic Currency ("₣ "), a blockchain-based electronic currency reflecting the value of a basket of primary national currencies. The IMF adopted it in 2031 to establish an international medium of exchange to end disputes about manipulation of values among the US Dollar, Euro, Yuan, Won, Yen, and Rupee

Greenhouse Gases, primarily carbon dioxide (CO_2), also trace amounts of methane (CH_4) ["natural gas" is 85% methane], CFCs, HCFCs, nitric acid, and water vapor

MSTY — "Multiple Interoperative System, Tier Y" computer, the SSPC supercomputer that provides computational support for all operations and monitors all mechanical functions.

NSSI	Network Security Systems, Incorporated, a client of CDI, run by Jordan Milhaus and Christopher Kangata
SMS	UN Security Management Services, providing security services to all UN System Agencies as part of the UN Department of Safety and Security.
SSP	Solar Shield Project, a set of 480 large mirrors in space to reflect sunlight into space and increase Earth's effective albedo while creating shaded areas on Earth's surface. The UN authorized it in 2027 to replace the unauthorized "tropospheric veil" system based on drones releasing chemicals in the tropopause
SSPC	UN Space Shield Project Command, created to operate the Solar Shield Project
UN	United Nations

MAIN CHARACTERS

Yazeen Abdulla	(aka Ahmed Alkoran or Mashad Anwar) ("he") member of the NSSI staff, reformed ISIS member
Sanjay Bhattachar	Jay ("he") SSPC Officer, Executive Assistant to Commander Fauré, born in Assam in 2001, moved to Canada as a child, served in the Canadian Air Force. Divorced, two boys.
Cai Jin	Cai ("she") computer systems whiz kid for the Chinese Air Force, co-founder and lead co-partner CDI
Natan Carmell	Natan ("he") computer technician at SMS, assisting Cheng Yiming on tracking down hackers
Cheng Yiming	Cheng ("he") Investigator for SMS
Robert Fauré	Commander ("he") head of the SSPC, former Canadian Navy Rear Admiral and pilot
Hua Luo Dan	Hua ("he") Junior partner in CDI
Mohamed Ibrahim	Ibrahim ("he") World Bank Vice President, former Ambassador for

	Maldives; "tropospheric veil project" creator in the 2020s
Christopher Kangata	Chris ("he") (aka Jomo Kahinde), allegedly an employee of the SSPC IT department, coordinating a cybersecurity contract with NSSI
Valery Malkovich	Malkovich ("he") Member, SSPC Board of Directors, employee of the UN Secretariat from Russia
Jordan Milhous	(aka Charles Morgan) ("he") NSSI's President
Kelly O'Rourke	("Kelly" "she") SSPC Officer, on assignment from the Irish Air Force, single. Born in Dublin, 2004.
Jerry Stephens	Stephens ("he") SSPC IT Director
Isaac Swerdling	("he") President, FirstWorld Bank
Yi Gong	Yi ("she") Junior partner in CDI
Wang Shu	Wang ("she") Director of UN SMS; from Singapore, worked with Ibrahim," from Singapore
Wei Tong	Wei ("he") Junior partner in CDI
Zhang Xingwen	("he") computer systems whiz kid for the Chinese Air Force, co-founder and partner in CDI

ABOUT THE AUTHOR

SAM BLEICHER is an Adjunct Law Professor at Georgetown University Law School in Washington DC. From 2014 to 2018, he served as a Member and Vice-Chair of the Virginia Air Pollution Control Board. He is a graduate of Harvard Law School and Northwestern University, Phi Beta Kappa with Honors in Economics.

His novels draw on his experience as a law firm partner and lobbyist; a senior official in the US Department of State, the US National Oceanic & Atmospheric Administration, and the Ohio EPA; as a law professor in the US; and as a visiting law professor in Russia and China.

Guardians of the Solar Shield is his third novel. His two earlier novels, *THE PLOT TO COOL THE PLANET, A Novel* (Newman Springs, 2d Printing 2019), and *APPOINTMENTS: A Novel of Politics in Our Nation's Capital* (2013), are available on Amazon and at local bookstores.

ACKNOWLEDGEMENTS

Special appreciation goes to **Maris St. Cyr**, my companion, for her sorely-tested patience and resilient emotional support, in addition to her creative editorial suggestions and critiques of draft after draft that no one else ever saw (for good reason.)

Warm thanks go to the many people who helped me improve various versions of the manuscript. Their ideas and insights made this book dramatically better. I list here those I recall, in alphabetical order: **Carol Bogash**, **Suzanne Conrad, Gregg Lehne, Bette Jafek Rosse**, and **Mary K. Zeravleff**, who all read at least one version of the manuscript and gave me valuable suggestions for improvements, from reordering chapters to reimagining characters.

My son, **Leo S. Bleicher**, gave me technical insights that led me to a more realistic understanding of the science of orbiting mirrors.

Of course, none of them bear any responsibility for the final product. For better or worse, I made the editorial decisions, from punctuation to plot.

Made in the USA
Middletown, DE
20 April 2021